D0561111

The People Down South

ILLINOIS SHORT FICTION

A list of books in the series appears at the end of this volume.

Cary C. Holladay

The People
Down South

UNIVERSITY OF ILLINOIS PRESS

Urbana and Chicago

Short Story Index
1989-1993

Publication of this work was supported in part
by grants from the Illinois Arts Council, a state agency.

This book is printed on acid-free paper.

"Keepers," *Missouri Review* (Fall 1981)
"The People Down South," *O. Henry Festival Stories: 1989*
  (Greensboro, N.C.: Trans-Verse Press, 1989)
"A Neighborhood Story," *Shore Writers' Sampler* (1987)
"Malta Fever," *Antietam Review* (1989)
"Out There," *Inlet* (Fall 1985)
"News from China," *Shore Writers' Sampler II* (1988)

Library of Congress Cataloging-in-Publication Data

Holladay, Cary C., 1958–
    The people down South / Cary C. Holladay.
        p.   cm.—(Illinois short fiction)
    ISBN 0-252-01668-8
    I. Title.   II. Series.
    PS3558.O347777P4   1989
    813'.54—dc19   89-31424
                                           CIP

To M. G. L.

Contents

Keepers   1

The People Down South   11

County of Rage, County of Young
Green Growing Things   25

To Ashes   32

Squabs   39

Smoketown Road   44

A Neighborhood Story   51

Under Glass   56

The Things That Scare Us   64

Malta Fever   75

Out There   82

Hetty Hawken   89

News from China 103

Yard Sale 116

Eva's Lover 128

Keepers

With a name like Emory he should never have left the South. Growing up in Mobile had almost been enough. The summer he was seventeen he decided to see it all before he left it. He drove all over the states and slept in the car. Some mornings he woke at sunrise not knowing where he was, with his arms flung over his head and crossed at the wrists as if bound. Then his mind would say Carolina or Georgia or Kentucky, and he'd turn back onto the highway a little east or a little west, but always north. He was running out of money by the time he got to Virginia, and then outside a bar in Roanoke two black boys fought him and took his wallet and his watch and the cheap ring that they thought was gold. He still had a little money hidden in the glove compartment of the car. The bruised jaw hurt him, but he laughed when he thought of the black boys trying to sell the old tin alloy ring for gold. Somewhere between Culpeper and Manassas his car broke down, the radiator boiling over, the engine hissing in the cricket-filled twilight. Red clay farmland stretched round him. He knew the car and knew there was nothing to be done, so he pulled his sack of belongings out of the back seat and flung the pale hair out of his eyes and put out his thumb.

He'd hitchhiked before, but he'd always been picked up by singles—once by a woman. A horse trailer and a pickup truck spun past him. Then a sports car pulled over, and he leaned down to the window and the driver asked where he was headed and he just said North. The woman in the passenger seat climbed out so he could

fold his thin six-foot frame into the back. Then they were back on
the highway, and Emory saw that the man was Chinese, with his
hair grown out long, and he wore an unironed white shirt with the
cuffs rolled back, and a pair of aviator sunglasses on top of his
head. The woman was beautiful in an odd way, very high cheekbones like a Slav, and hair like wet bark. The man drove very fast.
Once the woman warned him about the radar speed-checking, but
he didn't answer her; instead he lit a cigarette. Emory stared at the
backs of their necks. They told him they were going to New York,
and he thought they meant New York City, and he said that was
fine, and after they'd gone a hundred miles the woman said something about the Catskills, so he knew it wasn't the city, but that
was fine too.

They stopped at a pancake house for supper. Emory counted out
his money slowly in his hand. The woman saw him and said something to the man and the man said he would pay for Emory's
meal. Emory hadn't eaten for a day and a half. He ordered a stack
of pancakes and bacon and a plate of fried potatoes. The man and
his wife ordered ribeye steaks and then the man excused himself
and went to a telephone. He pushed some coins through the slot
and dialed, turning away while he talked. The woman smiled
across her steak and coffee at Emory and said her name was
Sloane, and her husband was Marty Chung, you know, whose pictures maybe he'd seen in the national weekly news magazines?
Emory had seen cameras on the back seat of the car, but he didn't
know the name. He told her he hadn't been able to read the magazines since he'd been on the road; the truth was he never read
them. The woman's eyes glowed, giving off light in a way he'd
never seen before. He wanted to tell her that she was beautiful but
found himself rubbing his sore jaw instead, and looking toward
Marty Chung on the telephone.

"Marty's been working too hard," Sloane said. "We went to Virginia to take pictures of the farms there. He always shoots in black
and white. Barns, silos, fields, acres foreshortened by angle."

If she'd asked Emory about himself, he would have told her
what there was to tell: how he didn't get along with his father and

how there were five younger brothers and sisters for his mother to take care of, and his father brought home enough money from the textile factory, but he brought it home in hard hands that hurt Emory. Emory had almost finished high school. At first he thought he'd just go to Birmingham and work in a steel mill, or the railroad yard. He loved the sound of trains. But he decided to go north because he wanted to see snow.

Now it was July. Even in the north it would be a long time before snow.

Marty Chung hung up the phone and slid into the vinyl booth beside his wife.

"I've been telling Emory about the farms," she said.

"Estep wants the set by Monday," said Marty, his mouth curling down.

"What did you tell him?"

Marty's reply made Emory want to laugh because it was street language, but the man's face was dark and he didn't dare. He wondered why the couple burdened themselves with him. The pancakes tasted good; his hollow stomach warmed with the food. They ate in silence for a while and then Emory tried to thank Marty Chung for the ride and the meal, but the man brushed aside his thanks. "Hitchhikers aren't supposed to be so polite. You ought to at least try to rape my wife."

Sloane laughed; Emory flushed. He ducked his head and poured honey on the last thick portions of pancake.

Marty Chung leaned across the table and put a hand on his arm. "If you come with us, you can have all the honey you want. Sloane's dad's a beekeeper."

The woman showed surprise, but Marty said to her, "Your father needs somebody to help around. Do odd jobs. What do you say, Emerson? Will you come with us?"

He said, "My name is Emory," and then, "I've never been to the Catskills before," and then, "Yes, I'll go."

When he had been alone on the road, driving his own car and getting into the fight in Roanoke, he'd felt powerful. Now, facing the Chinese photographer and his wife, he felt that something had changed hands. He didn't know what it was. He thought of his abandoned car sitting along the berm, cooling, cold, the dead waves of a Manassas radio station caught in the vents. And he wanted to go to the Catskills.

At first his heart beat fast from nervousness whenever he was near Marty or Sloane or Sloane's father, but once he became accustomed to them, he relaxed. At first the old man wouldn't let him go near the hives. He made Emory cook for them. Emory didn't mind; he was glad for the work. He loved making breakfast for Sloane: he served her the dark gold honey in a cup and told her how it tasted wild to him, like wild clover. Marty never rose before noon, and then he came down to the kitchen and drank a cup of coffee and went outside to greet his weimaraner. The dog would shake its short gray coat and turn its lavender stare upon its master. Emory liked cooking for them. At first he was afraid he would burn everything, that the meals wouldn't be right. But he'd worked one summer as a short-order cook at a restaurant in Mobile and he remembered what he'd learned, so everything turned out the way it was supposed to. He sat with the others at meals. Sometimes Marty Chung wanted a tray in his room, and it was always Sloane who took it up to him. Marty's photographs covered the walls of the old farmhouse, in wooden and acrylic frames that Sloane lovingly polished.

Then the beekeeper wanted Emory to start with the hives. Tented with veils, they moved among the humming structures. The first day Emory was stung four times.

"You'll become immune after a while," Sloane's father said.

Emory looked at his welts. How the bees fought their enemies, the big moving white hands, the scent and the violation maddening them to spurt their poison into the pillowed palms, the ridged knuckles, the areas where tiny hairs broke the surface over buried veins. The old man told him gloves were no good.

Sloane showed him how to pack the wounds with a paste of baking soda and water. "When they start to itch, that means they're getting better."

"I know that," he said, then wished he hadn't sounded angry.

"Do you miss Mobile?" she asked him once, for by now he'd told her about his growing up. He shook his head no. His childhood and early adolescence, summed up in a few sentences, became a myth to him.

These things felt real to him now: the meals at eight and noon and seven, and the room they gave him, on the first floor next to the kitchen, and the honeycombs dripping stickily, and the walks he took in the afternoons, up to the top of a hill where he could see a highway down below, on Fridays clogged with weekend traffic, people pouring out of New York City. Once he went on a longer hike into the steep mountains, where stone walls spiked with rocks paralleled the roads, and he saw that the hills were alive with people: picnickers and campers and even an old Iroquois whom Sloane had told him about.

The old beekeeper, his sloped spine covered with nets, his eyes watchful, spoke in a strong voice, like a wire being plucked. When Emory had been there five weeks, the old man made him write to his family in Alabama telling them where he was and that he was all right. Emory wondered if he would have written if the man hadn't told him to.

It was Marty who'd hired him, but Marty rarely spoke to him, except to say good morning. Marty photographed the beehives for an apiary magazine; he took his floral-eyed dog for runs; he walked in his sleep. The first time Emory heard him fumbling in the dark he was afraid. He called out, Who's there? and received no answer—only his own echoing southern accent and his breathing and Marty's breathing filling the black air of the kitchen. The next day he asked Sloane about it and she told him Marty never remembered. She looked about to cry, so he never mentioned it again. Some mornings he found Marty lying on the living room couch, or on the floor, or on the sunporch where Sloane had artfully hung baskets of coleus and philodendron. Emory would hear Marty coming awake, yawning and sighing, in the early morning. When he walked, he found his way round the dark rooms with the easy stalking gait of a night creature in a jungle. Once Emory found him asleep with a Nikon in his arms, clad as usual in his old jeans.

During the day Sloane sang around the house, helped Marty in his darkroom, cataloged his photographs, read books in a hammock strung from two backyard oaks. The telephone rang a dozen times a day for Marty; he curled it between his neck and shoulder while he spoke to editors and agents in a kind of shorthand, quick phrases, promises, evasions. His tone was the same with everyone, as if he spoke to the same person each time. Emory decided that Marty liked—or disliked—all of his callers equally. One night Sloane received a long-distance call from Seattle, and Emory heard her saying, Oh Peter! Oh Peter! in a delighted way, and afterward she and Marty argued late into the night, alternately sharp and raging with one another on the sunporch, until Emory fell asleep. When he woke he found two whiskey glasses and a half-bottle of Scotch pooled with the melted ice from an overturned ice bucket, all on a tray. He wondered who Peter was and if Sloane and Marty always drank when they argued. He never saw them drink otherwise.

The next day Marty went down to New York for the weekend. Sloane fretted like a child, but her blue eyes were cold. "He didn't need to go away," she said. "Of course he has to travel with his work, but this trip is just to punish me."

Her father, mending a bee net, asked, "Why didn't you just go with him?" Sloane rose from the table with a strangled sob, threw her napkin down, and ran from the room.

Both nights that weekend Emory thought about Sloane alone in the room she shared with Marty. He wanted to go to her. But he didn't dare: maybe Marty was still there after all, crouched behind a bureau or smoking in bed, his long black hair fanning out on the pillow. Where would he go in New York, what would he do? Emory had never seen the city, but he could imagine Marty in cramped candle-lit rooms speaking in his telephone code to faceless serious others with ambitions like his own. The previous week he'd had two photographs of the president in the news magazine with the largest nationwide circulation. As usual, Sloane framed the glossies. When she hung them in the foyer, Marty chided her for her patriotism: "I have no patience with that emotion."

On Sunday afternoon Peter from Seattle called again. On Sunday evening Marty returned with eleven rolls of film to be developed. He and Sloane worked on them late into the night, and they seemed very happy together. Emory thought, I could have gone to her. It's good that I didn't, but I could have. He rubbed his itching palms together. His mother used to say, If your left palm itches, means you're gonna travel. Right palm means you're gonna kiss a fool. But she hadn't been talking about beestings.

August, the dry gold husk of summer, ended: to Emory, accustomed to southern heat, the season was comfortable, but the old man and Sloane and Marty said all day long how hot, how hot. Sloane lay like a lazy cat in her hammock, with Marty in a lawn chair by her feet. The old man and Emory gathered the honey.

"The hive is like a brain," the beekeeper said, and Emory thought his face looked very red—"with every insect doing what it should, all the parts working for the whole, or else the hive is like a body, and the queen is the brain, and she makes all the decisions and the others follow by instinct." Something in his voice warned Emory. The old man clutched his chest and fell heavily against a hive, upsetting it, the bees swarming out in a furious winged wave, pelting the old man, who toppled to the ground in a tangle of nets and limbs. With a cry, Emory lifted him by the shoulders and dragged him clear of the bees. He did not feel his own stings. Marty sprinted toward them: Emory realized he'd never seen him run before. Together they carried Sloane's father back to the house. At first Sloane didn't understand that he was dead; she kept thinking he had fainted because of the stings. Then Marty went to the telephone and Sloane went to Emory and leaned her head against his chest. His heart rocked inside him. His scalp puffed and burned from stings. He said nothing, but he held her.

"He worked so hard," she said. "Marty would have supported him completely, but he wouldn't hear of it. All his life, he worked so hard."

The funeral drew more mourners than Emory had expected, but most of them were friends of Marty's who'd come up from the city. Sloane whispered to Emory, "I don't know any of these people," and later, "We're the only family he has." The old man was buried in a tiny cemetery on a hilltop. During the final prayer Emory raised his head and looked into the Catskills as if he were seeing them for the first time. Far away he saw a hang glider, taking the cold high currents of the air; then it dropped, and his heart spiraled downward with it. Had it crashed in a field some-where, miles away? Or splintered against a mountain? His throat went dry. He wanted to tell Sloane about it. But by the time the prayer was over he wondered if he had even seen the glider. Maybe the pilot was in control after all.

After the ceremony Marty steered both Sloane and Emory back toward the car. It was the first time Marty had intentionally touched him since the time in the restaurant when he'd put his hand on Emory's arm and asked him to come with them. The con-tact maddened Emory; he wanted to shake it off. When they re-turned to the farmhouse, there were a dozen cars in the driveway. Emory had never been to a funeral before, so he didn't know about the visiting afterward. Before they got out of the car, Sloane said to Marty, "Oh, make them go away! I don't want to see anybody!" and Marty's face assumed its dark, angry look.

Sloane wore a silk cocktail dress, the only black garment she owned. Marty had loaned Emory a black jacket, too narrow in the shoulders, too short in the arms, so that Emory could only carry it instead of wearing it. Marty played with the cuffs of his unironed white shirt and said, "They won't be here very long." Sloane got out of the car and ran inside.

"They'll be wanting drinks," Marty told Emory. He led him into the kitchen, through the unfamiliar crowd, and directed him to mix whiskey and soda for those who wanted it. A red-faced man handed Marty a bottle of rum in a paper bag and winked at him. Marty thanked him with a nod. Emory looked for Sloane, but she had disappeared. Once he caught a glimpse of her in a doorway, but when he looked again she was gone. The red-faced man asked for a refill and Emory jumped. He wanted a drink him-self, but he was afraid Marty would see him drinking and be angry.

By midevening all the others had gone home. Emory collected the sticky glasses from the tables and the arms of chairs and washed them in the kitchen sink. He saw Marty sitting in a wicker chair in the sunroom, but he didn't know where Sloane was. His heart felt as big as the silent house. The plan formed slowly in his mind, so slowly that he didn't even realize it was a plan until midnight, when he lay on his cot and smelled the smoke from Marty's cigarette and clenched the sheet between his hands. He thought how he would wait two hours, three, until he knew Marty was asleep. Once he thought he heard the slow scraping sound of Marty's sleep-numb feet on the stairs, navigating, some watchful lobe of his brain counting the steps, warning him of corners, but Emory told himself, No, it's only the wind.

Or the leaves of trees: the hours stretched by, ticking with the tick of black elm leaves against the window. Still Marty sat on the sunporch with the drink in his hand and the wisp of smoke about his head. At four o'clock Emory went to look at him and found him fast asleep, sitting up, the glass curved in against his knee in a fragile balance. Emory removed the glass so it wouldn't fall to the floor if Marty stirred.

He thought of Sloane lying upstairs and his heart raced. As he mounted the stairs he thought, Sleeping and sleepwalking are like being blind, with senses making up for one another. In Mobile he'd lived next door to a blind woman. Sometimes he would try to cover his eyes with his arms or a towel to block out images and light, to see how she saw. He thought about the blind woman as he climbed the stairs, his hand damp on the banister, and he felt as if a thick towel mantled his eyes. He thought of the half-empty whiskey bottle the night Marty and Sloane had argued so late and so long, and of Marty now sleeping off his liquor.

He turned down the hallway and found himself at the doorway to her room. Bars of moonlight fell across the floor from the unshaded window. He saw the neatly made bed, the open closet doors, the bureau drawers spilling clothes. She was gone.

Gone. He looked out the window and saw the empty driveway and imagined Sloane in the sports car somewhere on the dark highway with her hair flying out behind her. He thought, She left with the others, so I didn't hear the tires on the gravel.

Marty's hand was on his back. He felt the warmth, the pressure of his fingers, but he had not heard him climb the stairs or pad down the hallway. His own breath caught in his lungs, hot and thick, and his hands coiled into fists. He didn't know how long he stood there with his spine stiff and the moonlight flaring. He smelled Marty's smell of smoke and liquor and sleep, and he moved his feet slowly, so slowly, until the hand no longer touched his back and Marty made his way across the room to the bed and lay there with his arms spread out like wings. His black hair fell across his neck and Emory thought, He doesn't know.

By sunrise Emory was on the highway. He walked into the cool breeze, past the hill where Sloane's father lay in his grave. All around shimmered the green mountains, but Emory couldn't smell their tree scent; his nostrils still held the odor of his own fearful sweat from the touch of Marty Chung's hand. He pictured Marty waking at noon in the empty house and Sloane arriving somewhere with blue-circled eyes and sad raging words.

A truck pulled over. Emory climbed in and said he was heading north. The driver spoke out of the side of his mouth: Montreal. Emory thought he would like to see Canada. They passed a 'possum with gaping blood-throat: road kill. His life in the Catskills slid past him. Well, he would see snow. And Canada geese. He'd heard they covered the sky like darkness, flying over.

Marty would wake to his telephone and his cameras and his tense, silent dog with its hyacinth eyes. Would he know what to do about the hives when the seasons changed? Emory had never seen him work with the bees. What happened to them in autumn, or in snow?

The driver was asking him where he was from, with that drawl. Mobile, said Emory. He couldn't call his mother's face to mind. Or Sloane's. Maybe Marty would free the bees. Or were they already free? What happens next? Sloane's father had never told him what beekeepers must do for bees during the winter, or what the bees did for themselves.

The People Down South

Once she was pretty, with big breasts and long legs as smooth and well balanced as the barrel of a gun, so good looking he found it hard to breathe around her, left his wife for her. They had a few perfect years and a few that were all right and then, after ten years had gone by, he wondered when she'd grown so heavy, when her face had lost its power over him. Now her trademark blue eyeshadow made her eyes look old. At least she hadn't cut her hair, and she still set a good table: ham, slaw, cornbread, lemon pie, plain iced cake, and punch that he said was too sweet but she always put extra sugar in her own glass and even then said it wasn't sweet enough for her.

Horace Kimball and Juneal Wailes were not married. At first she talked about it, but that had stopped a long time ago, stopped even when their bodies seemed made for good times. Not being married didn't matter. After all, he'd left his wife for her. He made good money as a backhoe operator. And the house was Juneal's, she owned it. Her grandfather had built it a long time ago, right there on the straightaway of the river, a fine spot, with a cool breeze coming off the water, and birds ruling the marsh on the other shore. It didn't matter that the paint was chipping or that the floors slanted inside or that the stairway had a little sag in it. The house was just settling, even after this many years.

Now it took a mountain to move Juneal. She sat in the yard looking out at the river. Boats went by, big slow barges and swift speedboats sticking halfway out of the water, and she waved at the people on the boats until it was dark and the river was empty. Theirs was the last house on the road. Cornfields lay between their place and the nearest neighbor. It was a summer without rain, and the stalks stood dry and brown as paper bags. During the day Juneal worked with her candle-making things, but not much: "What another person would take a week to do, I can do in a day." And then in the evening she watched the boats.

Horace had to look for bodies that summer. A man had bought a big piece of land and wanted to put a plywood mill on it, but the land was old and the plat showed that it had three graves on it, exact locations unknown. State law said the man had to find those bodies and dig them up and rebury them under concrete with a little chain-link fence around them, right there on the same land. The state would somehow know if the man didn't look hard enough and didn't rebury the bodies, and then there'd be trouble. The man explained this to Horace.

"Who the hell are these dead guys," the man said. "The South has so many dead bodies lying around, they could be slaves or old soldiers or just drifters or niggers in modern life that nobody gave a damn about, that died from the heat." Whenever he mentioned the heat, he cursed it. He was from Rhode Island. Horace asked what body of water was around that island, but the man never did answer. He was short and ugly and mean, and he talked funny. He'd point and say, "Look at that big hock," meaning hawk.

So Horace had to take his backhoe and dig up all this land. It hurt to see topsoil flying away in the wind, good soil frizzling into dust, but the pay was good and now he was eager to find those dead people. Big chunks of earth reared up in the teeth of the backhoe. He went all the way down to the clay. There were no clues at all about where the bodies were, or when they'd died, but ripping up acres was steady work, and the man was easy to work for because he only came around for a little while every day and he paid Horace in cash.

Juneal listened about the search with her eyes far off like she was dreaming. "Could be a family graveyard, could be nobody. Somebody from a long time ago could be playing a trick on that man. What if you don't find 'em?"

"I'll find 'em," said Horace. He pictured fine strong people sitting up in the dirt, shaking grit from their eyes, thanking him.

"Maybe there'll be a treasure with them, a gold bracelet or a wallet full of money," said Juneal.

Horace reached back in his memory for stories that old folks had told him, trying to recall talk of dead rebels or people who'd disappeared, but he came up empty.

"I don't believe anybody just disappears, ever," he said.

"But they do," said Juneal, stirring pink wax in a big pot, adding a few drops of a special oil to make it smell like strawberries. A gift shop in town sold the candles she made. She molded them into the shapes of mushrooms, apples, and pyramids. The extra income was nice to have.

When he left for work in the early morning she was still asleep, but she had packed his lunch the night before. He loved mornings because of the birds singing and the thin current of coolness in the air, before it turned hot. He leaned against the open doorway, eating his breakfast, watching a spider link its threads among boxwood leaves. Whatever did she do all day, if she didn't make candles, and who did she see, nobody? Used to be, the house was their hideaway from his wife, and nobody else belonged in their world. His world was the back of Juneal's neck, when her hair was coiled up and she was making coffee. Their world was the warmth they made together when thunderstorms turned the river rough and black outside.

But now he was lonely. He remembered the last time they'd laughed together, really laughed: back in the winter, when it snowed real deep, deeper than they'd ever seen before. He'd had a yellow hound then. From the window they'd watched the dog running round and round in the snow, looking for a place to pee, knocked for a loop by the hidden landscape. They'd laughed themselves silly over that.

The snow melted, the yellow hound ran away, daffodils bloomed madly in skewed rows near the clothesline. Juneal said, "My grandmother was a somebody. Knew the names of all sorts of flowers, and it bored me to death. Even now, I'm glad to just be able to look at the flowers and not hear about those damn Latin names.'' Horace thought that was odd, because Juneal liked indoor-type plants and kept a bunch of hanging baskets filled with thick-leafed, thirsty ones that never bloomed. Summertime came, and tiger lilies took the place of the daffodils. Juneal fried eggplant, read magazines, started burning candles on a card table beside her when she sat out at night.

"Keeping bugs away?" he asked, pulling off his T-shirt and wiping his face with it.

"I want to be a lighthouse lady."

"To guard against wrecks? Nobody'll hit here, it's straight."

Something about the horizon at night did things to him, right in his heart. Downriver, the water curved into a vanishing point. Gulls dove for fish. The sky right above the water was white, and above that, in a strip above the marsh reeds, it was dark as grapes. He pictured himself and Juneal throwing a party, playing harmonicas, shucking corn, wrestling gators, mating with fifty guests. Once, Juneal had baked a pan of marijuana brownies, and they were damn good. It all wears out, he thought.

"I saw your wife today," Juneal said. They never called her by her name, Kathy. "In that junk shop I like to go to. She was looking at a rug that smelled bad because it had been in a flood. Her bra strap kept falling down. She didn't say hi."

"Did you buy anything?"

"There was a TV set that a kid was watching a monster show on, and I wanted it, but the lady said it wasn't for sale. There was a little sewing table I liked, but two fat women bought it before I could get my hands on it. I pulled a book off the shelf that I thought was called "Crapbook," but it turned out it said "Scrapbook." So I didn't buy anything, and neither did your wife."

He chuckled, but she didn't. He sat down beside her, picked up a candle in its glass holder, closed his eyes and smelled its lemon scent. "What would you like to do, if you didn't live here and make candles?"

"I'd like to do the voices for cartoon characters. Or live on a houseboat and eat butterscotch pie all day."

"Would I be on that houseboat with you?"

In profile, her chin had almost disappeared into her fleshy neck, and her shoulders strained forward as if she were riding a bicycle. His heart ached for how pretty she used to be. Her breath was as bad as a cat's. "I know a lot of people on boats," she said. "The ones who wave to me. They know me now."

"I guess you've watched them enough to know."

She turned her head and looked him straight in the eye. "Your wife looked fed up."

"Like how?"

"Like she wanted to burn that store down."

The wind shifted, a whippoorwill called, the tide rose. He sat out with Juneal a while longer, and then he went inside.

Once, Kathy had told him, "You're one of those people who lives from obsession to obsession." Kathy read psychology books and bugged him to tell her about his dreams. She loved to talk about hers, but he said dreams were the most boring thing he could think of. Obsessions, though, were another matter. Mostly they were obsessions he had to hide from her, like his feelings for Juneal. He'd been drifting along in marriage with Kathy, Kathy who spent all her time strumming a guitar and tuning it too tight, so the strings snapped and hit her in the face. She was always down in the dumps about this or that, and always doing things to her hair, until she ended up with a hairdo like every other woman's: hard, burned-looking curls in a helmet shape. And she always wanted something from him: what she called "response." She'd show him a picture in a psychology magazine, just a bunch of scrawled lines, and say, "Look, an elephant drew that. It held a piece of chalk in its foot and actually did that." He'd say, "Hot damn," which was never enough; Kathy wanted more.

But Juneal. One day he'd looked up from cashing a check at the bank and there she was at the next teller's window, turning in a pillowcase full of loose change. He struck up a conversation about how many pennies she had saved.

"Law, I don't know. Couple thousand." She smiled, slow and shy and gorgeous.

"And how many dimes?"

The teller interrupted, "I really don't have time to count all this right *now*. You can count it yourself with a machine we have in the back."

"You've got to count it now," Horace told the teller. "She needs that pillowcase to lay her pretty head on tonight."

The teller (he was in Kathy's exercise class and she'd reported that he was one of those fairy-men; when the rest of the class took a break, the teller lay on his back writing the alphabet in the air with his toes) stepped out from behind his cubicle, jingled a big silver keyring, and let Juneal into a little room where the counting machine was. Horace followed them, and nobody told him to leave. The teller departed. That very night, the pillowcase was back on Juneal's pillow, and Juneal and Horace were kicking the slats out of the bed. He couldn't believe he'd found a beautiful girl, with a house all her own, who liked him.

When he got home the next morning, Kathy announced, "We're at war." She plucked a deep string on her guitar, for emphasis. She served him charred hot dogs, a tomato with flies on it, and bread gone blue with mold. He went over to Juneal's and ate fried chicken and black-eyed peas with extra molasses. The next few weeks passed in a heady excitement, as Kathy attempted alternately to punish him and to woo him back, and all Juneal did was open her arms and let him love her.

All that lovely dark hair, and that slim figure (whereas Kathy had gone to lumps and strings) and not married, simply because she hadn't found the right man yet and after all had a house of her own. He moved in with her and they were happy, but he never got around to divorcing Kathy, so a couple of years ago she divorced him. For a long time that made it more exciting, to leave Kathy as a loose end dangling from his old life. He vowed he'd never marry again, because sex was better that way. And then one day he looked at Juneal and saw a fat squaw, sad and bitter and quiet, and he wondered just what had happened to that beautiful girl.

At last he found a bone. It slid through the teeth of the backhoe and fell back into the earth. He stopped the machine and clawed through the dirt to find it again. It was old and porous, not a bit of skin left on it. He marked the spot with a big stick and called the Rhode Island man, and together they dug with shovels and hoes, as mosquitoes chewed them into all-over welts.

"This can count as one body, even if we don't find the rest of it," the man said.

"Looks like a dog or a deer bone," said Horace. "I'm not a doctor, so I wouldn't know for sure, but—"

"No, you don't know for sure. The state'll get their first cement grave out of this bone." The man stuck his hoe into the ground, picked up the bone, and held it between his arms as if measuring. He pulled off his cap and wiped his cheek on his shoulder. "This evil *heat*." He tossed the bone on the floor of his car.

That evening Horace said to Juneal, "But it's not a person, I can tell. I've see enough animal bones to know."

"Does it matter? All he wants is to find 'em."

"It doesn't seem right, to bury an animal bone under a cement slab and say it's a person."

"Are you afraid a big hand will come down from the sky and knock you over? God doesn't care what goes on with those old bones."

"I take my work seriously, is all."

"Make the work last; that man's rich."

"Don't eat so many rolls, Juneal, you don't need rolls and butter and all that sugar in your drink."

She pulled her hand away from the basket of rolls as if he'd slapped her, tears filming her black eyes. "I'm sick of you, Horace, you just make me feel bad."

He got up from his chair and went around the table, tender toward her for the first time in many months. "Don't cry." He hugged her, but her scalp smelled so strongly of sebum that he drew back, repulsed.

Her tears did dry, and she was calm again, as if she were watching him on TV with her mind on something else. "I've met somebody," she said. "I met him at the grocery store. He wants to see me, but where does that leave me? I'm not married, but I'm sure not single." Deliberately she reached for a roll and bit into it, gazing at him defiantly while she chewed, her cheeks blown out like a toad's belly.

Strange, but he'd half-expected this. Tremors of mutiny had reached him even as he knelt in the field that morning with the bone in his hands.

"So you want to go sparkin'? Fine with me," but the words were dust in his mouth. He wasn't sure he believed her.

"We've never married, we've never talked about having a child. All we talk about is your work." She stood and cleared the table, stacking the plates and carrying them to the sink. As she scraped them, washed them, and put them back in the corner cupboard, he stood in the doorway rocking back and forth on his flat feet. "If I kick you out of this house, you'll have to find a place of your own. You can't go back to Kathy."

"What do you mean?" She'd read his mind: as if Kathy would have him. His heart started to jackhammer in his chest.

"She's getting married again. Her engagement was in the paper." With a wet towel Juneal swabbed the stove, then slapped the towel triumphantly on the kitchen counter. "She doesn't love you anymore, hasn't for a long time, and neither do I."

"Juneal, don't say this! We can make it work. We've just been distracted lately, is all, so please don't start with somebody else." He meant it. He just hadn't known that being together would mean going on and on, even when there wasn't much to say and when the fine glow of love had evaporated like rain on hot blacktop. He put his arms around her and touched her in the old way, though at first she didn't respond. He pressed up against her as she stood by the stove. He kept kissing her and speaking low words into the heavy fall of her hair. A smear of butter gleamed on her chin, but he concentrated on the light in her eyes when at last she sighed and let him take her.

Out of the blue, the man said he wasn't working fast enough. "You're costing me too much money," he said. "This whole thing stinks."

"I can either be careful and look for these bodies like you asked me to, or I can just mess up the ground and not look and not find anything.''

"Can't you just work faster?'' From Horace's high seat in the dozer, the man's eyes looked pale and cruel in his big face. Horace pictured the man pulling him down off the seat, kicking him in the head till he died, then hauling his remains to the state capital and saying, "Here's one.''

The man went on, "What I'm doing is a community service. This plywood mill will give people jobs, for God's sake. Up north they'd appreciate that. But here—hah!'' He gave a mirthless laugh. "Nobody wants to work down here. The buzzards work harder than the people do,'' and he gestured to distant shapes wheeling in the sky.

Horace's anger boiled over. He leaped down from the bulldozer and faced the man. "I go at my own pace, and I do good work. So stay out of my hair.''

To his surprise, the man backed off. He spat on the ground and turned and walked back to his car. Horace watched him drive off, trailing a funnel of dust on the road, and when his anger cooled, he started to work again, but the man's insults stayed with him, burrlike. He wasn't too slow, he wasn't, but a little voice said, Yes you are. The broad field lay behind him, its earth turned over and under, the past becoming the present. He went all the way down to the blue marl. Dig deeper than that, you'd find dinosaur eggs. A scattering of noontime shadows lay over the land. At last he stopped the bulldozer in mid-bite and took his lunch under an old shade tree with above-ground roots thick as his arm. In a paper bag Juneal had packed a bacon sandwich, a jam sandwich, a peach, the last one-fourth of a bag of potato chips, and a can of cola.

While he ate he thought about Kathy. When he'd started seeing Juneal, Kathy's curiosity got the better of her at last, and one evening, after he'd combed back his hair and brushed his teeth (it was one of his handsome nights, when his skin was all clear and his nose didn't look sharp-as-a-hatchet like Kathy was always saying), he'd strolled out the door of their mobile home and gotten into his car. An old Corvair, he had then. He drove over to Juneal's house happily, his mind filled with images of the two of them in her bed or on the rug in her living room, his body on fire all over. When he turned into the narrow road that ran down to the river, he saw the whole world with a clarity and a reverence like never before, all because Juneal was waiting for him with the high windows of her house all lit up.

He drove up and parked the car. Then something rustled behind him, right there in the car. It was Kathy. She had hidden herself under a coat in the back seat, and now she rose up to confront him.

"So it's Juneal Wailes," she said, her white face pinched and ugly in the rear-view mirror. At first he thought the dusk was playing tricks on him, but he whirled around just in time to catch Kathy's stinging slap on his cheek. "Now you can drive me the hell home," she said, and what could he do but obey?

Now she was getting married again. The old women in his family had a saying: "There never was a wedding where hearts weren't broken." He didn't know why he should care that Kathy was getting married again, but he did, and right there under the tree, licking jam off his thumb, he admitted it to himself. Strange that in a place that size they didn't run into each other more often. Juneal saw her everywhere she went, at least she claimed she did.

Time to get back to work. He stood and stretched. How had it happened that he had such lonely work? His other construction jobs had people around, lots of people. All this time alone couldn't be good. Maybe this was what had made Juneal get so funny, being by herself too much. She used to have friends, two bossy, prissy girls named Lucy and Sandy, who she'd gone to high school with. There was right much back and forth with Lucy and Sandy in the way of swapping recipes, giving advice on how to hem curtains, and talking about men. The recipes and sewing he tuned out, but the talk of men, carried on just within his earshot, was urgent and full of undercurrents and made Lucy and Sandy a bit more interesting. Was Juneal not friends with them anymore, or what? He hadn't seen them for ages. Then there was Mary Beth Book, who ran "Book's Nook," the gift shop where Juneal sold her candles. Mary Beth Book was middle aged and sophisticated. Her auburn hair had a white streak in it, and she once gave Juneal a pair of green leather gloves that were too small, but still Juneal was proud of the gloves. Juneal used to praise Mary Beth Book and the things in the shop, but no longer.

The sun was hotter than ever. He headed back to the backhoe, made his customary walk around the big machine, and then he saw it.

A ribcage. It was sticking up out of the ground, half-turned, the white bones like the fingers of a big hand. Breathless, he swooped down, unfastened it from the grip of the machinery, and cradled it in his arms. Miraculously, its hinges held together. With sweating hands he felt his own live ribs through his cotton shirt. This was a person, no doubt about it, a small person who had lived and died, whose ribs had held a heart, but of course the heart was gone. He laid the ribcage down, started the dozer, and very carefully backed it up a few yards. Then, on hands and knees, he sifted through every inch of that area, unearthing a veritable sheaf of bones, all short and delicate yet strong, the joints jigsawing together like nature meant them to. It was a small woman or a child, with not a bit of identification that he could see, no clothing or jewelry or anything that could give a name or a time. It was just a broken skeleton, the last physical reminder of a person. He found the skull last. Its sockets gazed wide at him, its upper teeth bore down on the lowers like his own teeth sometimes did at night, too hard, giving him headaches. The top of it had countless tiny cracks in it, like the crazing of glaze on old white china.

He took off his shirt and wrapped the bones in it, as stiff and exhausted as if he had dug up miles of peanuts. The sun said it was late afternoon. He would take the skeleton home, show it to Juneal, and call the man to say he'd found it.

When he came in sight of the house, he could see Juneal lugging something in her arms, then tossing whatever it was onto a heap down by the river. She didn't see him approaching, and when he reached the heap she had gone back inside.

It was a pile of her houseplants, a dense tangle of cultured vegetation: striped leaves like a green skunk; dried-out ferns; rootbound poinsettias evicted from their shallow pots; long, curling tendrils that had tinier plants attached to the ends.

Juneal came out and hurled another armload onto the pile. "I'm tired of taking care of them, but this way they get a fighting chance."

"Housecleaning?"

"You could call it that. They're not fun anymore."

The plants looked pitiful, jumbled together like garbage. They would all die. But he couldn't think about them, not when the shirt in his arms was a hammock for bones.

"Look," he said, spreading the shirt open on the ground, laying out the bones one by one. Juneal's gasp was gratifying. She put out a finger and touched a rib.

"I couldn't find quite all of it," he said.

"Could be old or young, black or white."

"It's young," he said. "I just know it."

He bundled the bones back up, went inside, and called the Rhode Island man at the local motel, but the phone just rang and rang. He waited a while, then tried again. When there was still no answer he put the bones in a bag, put his shirt back on, and started back to the field.

There was his backhoe, but how had it gotten moved? As he drew closer, he realized that there were two machines in the field—his was still where he'd left it, but there was another one, too. And there was Rhode Island, hands on hips, talking with a man named Renshaw. Horace had worked with Renshaw on other construction jobs. So someone else was being hired too, to make the work go faster. Well, it would be less lonely.

"Howdy," said Horace, but Renshaw looked down at his feet, and Rhode Island just said, "Where you been?"

Something in his tone made Horace tuck the sack of bones under his arm like all it had in it was a set of tools. The man said, "Well, this makes it easier for me, you taking off in the middle of the day like this. Go on home; I don't need you anymore."

"But I—"

"You heard me!" From his wallet he uncreased a few bills and thrust them at Horace. "Goddamn waste of money."

As Horace turned away he heard the man tell Renshaw, "Yep, graves. Start digging."

He put the sack carefully in the cab of the backhoe, started the engine, moved out on the road, and drove home. Cicadas made walls of sound on either side of the road, their drumming voices starting low and slow and scaling up loud and fast.

As soon as Juneal saw the sack, she said, "You mean you didn't give it to him?"

"It's mine."

"But it's his land."

"I'll bury it." By the time he found his shovel it was after dark. He started spading the soft ground.

Juneal protested, "I don't want that thing on my lawn." She brought her chair out and set up her candles on the card table, facing the river. "I'm expecting a visitor."

"Who?" Digging, Horace turned his head sideways to look at her. Like Christmas lights, the colorful candles glowed through their glass containers on the table.

"The man who wants to see me, the one I met at the grocery store. He owns a barge, goes right by here every night."

Horace tamped the ground over the small grave, saying nothing, feeling that he had rescued someone.

"You're welcome to join us," Juneal said over her shoulder.

"No, thanks." He put the shovel away, went inside, and read the paper. Lo and behold, there was Kathy's wedding picture. He didn't know her new husband. Her hat was so funny looking, at first he thought she was wearing a cake on her head.

It got late. Looking out the window, he saw Juneal's big shape slumped over at the card table, the lights flickering around her. She seemed to be asleep. There were no boats that he could see and no sound of tires on the road behind the house. The river gave off its breeze and its yellow smell. He went in the bedroom and tried to sleep, but all he could think of was that little set of bones.

A long time went by. He thought, I should go check on her; her hair could catch fire from those candles. He pictured flames racing up the long curtain of hair, lighting up the darkness, sheathing her in fire before she could scream. Then it would all end, and something new would begin.

But at last he got up and went outside and called her name.

County of Rage, County of Young Green Growing Things

This morning when I wake up, I think—first and always—of Ronnie Shoop. It's been two years now. Probably no one else thinks about him all the time, not even his pale little swaybacked scarecrow brother, Chet. Yes, surely Chet has achieved a merciful portion of forgetfulness by now; after all, he was only nine when Ronnie died.

Tomorrow will be the two-year anniversary of Ronnie's death. I live it again and again: I was driving out to Mrs. Anderson's greenhouse to buy something pretty for my apartment, something that could live in north light. It was a balmy winter day, lemon skied. I didn't look around enough; my eyes tunneled a path along the narrow road and all I thought about was flowers. The fields on either side of the road were a soft brown; I had nothing on my mind but flowers. The Anderson Home and greenhouse are out in the country, accessible only by a state road. I never saw Ronnie until that last bit part of a second, just as he rolled under the wheels, like a burrowing animal. The football he'd been chasing bounced off my windshield with the sound of a booted foot squinching on ice. I don't remember stopping the car, but I do remember crouching on the road tugging at this limp boy who was bleeding from the mouth. All I heard was my own ragged breathing. "Oh, oh, oh," I cried. "Help!" and then out of nowhere appeared a line of children. One of them must have thrown the football that the injured boy was chasing. I called, "Go get help! An ambulance, a doctor! Oh, I didn't mean to do it."

All those eyes on me, level as guns. An eternity later an ambulance arrived, Mrs. Anderson galloped across the field to scream at me, a state policeman opened the door of his car and hustled me inside. But it was all too late, because the boy had died while we were all alone, before anyone else came. I was the last person to see him alive. I killed him. He might have been governor, he might have been a murderer, but he never had time to grow up or fall in love or catch that football, because I crashed into him with a ton of Pontiac.

I should have been electrocuted, or at least put away for a long time, but they didn't even suspend my license. His death was ruled accidental. He lies in a corner grave in an old Baptist cemetery. Forever ten, he sleeps beneath a harsh new stone. I go to that cemetery often and sit by his grave and think about God. I don't know anything about God now, but when I was little I knew a lot. God lived in my backyard lilac bush. His kiss tasted of the rusty water from the old pump that I wasn't supposed to use, and when a sunset hurt your eyes, that was His stare.

Chet Shoop has $2,000 in his bank account now; it's the reason I live. He's used to my visits. I have all kinds of thoughts when I go to see him: wishing his brother had just been a squirrel, for example. Chet's closed face, with sleepers in the corners of his eyes and tassels of hair shaking over his ears, absolves me from guilt for a few sweet moments. Back at the scene of my crime, I can retreat to the blankness of my mind before the steering wheel rose in my hands like a mad thing. That sickening sensation of riding *over* something, of grinding against something soft with bones inside. Whenever I see Chet I'm conscious of veins, joints, sockets, tendons, his pinkish hairline. Not much chin: I should consult with an orthodontist about braces before his teeth are set for life.

Chet and I face each other in the living room of the Home. Incredible, but the new jacket I brought is too tight across his thin shoulders. "You've grown, Chet."

"I guess." He tugs at the sleeves.

"You're getting tall. Don't worry; I'll exchange this jacket for a bigger one. What else can I bring you, Chet?"

"It ain't Christmas. Ain't my birthday."

Doesn't he realize what tomorrow is? "I just like to bring you presents."

Why are the plants in this room always limp and brown stained, when Mrs. Anderson runs a greenhouse? A picture of Mary and Jesus covers part of a long crack in the wall. Jesus looks like a fat aardvark that's been skinned out of its shell. The long crack winds out of the top of Mary's head and ends in a teacup shape up by the ceiling. The sofa where I sit is dark and lumpy, like a baked sweet potato. I lean over to a doorknob (every doorknob in this house is thickly looped with rubber bands), pluck a band from the knob, and stretch it between my fingers.

"What else do you like, Chet?" He has to help me. I've brought clothes, books, games, paints, and toys, but now, after two years, I'm running out of ideas. The new TV set, there in the corner, is what I gave him for Christmas, but Mrs. Anderson won't allow TVs in the children's rooms, so it's out here for all to enjoy. That's even better. I want the others to know Chet's not alone. He has me.

"I like storms," he says. His eyes travel to the window. One thing about the Home, the windows are always ammonia clean. From where we sit Chet and I can see the other foster children playing beneath the shadows of enormous clouds. This is a day when you notice the clouds: they look like the clouds in wide-angle photographs taken in the 'thirties, all dark flat bottoms and the tops supporting whole pillowy cities. When I visit the Home, even ordinary things look different, like the birds. The sparrows here wear not feathers, but hard little platelets of armor.

"I like storms too. What is it about them that you like?"

He shrugs off the too-tight jacket and flips it back to me. I am careful not to touch his hands as I take it. We never touch. Once I tried to hug him and he stiffened like a pillar of salt. I've never seen him cry. I've told him to call me Nancy, or Miss Meade if he'd rather, but he doesn't call me anything. My friends say, Why don't you try to adopt him? But that wouldn't work, I know just what would happen; Chet would crawl behind my couch and hide there like a scared new cat, afraid to come out, silently hating me. For he does hate me, I think; he just hasn't realized it yet. Every time I visit, I search to discover signs of hatred in his skim-milk eyes. He's a fool not to hate me. I make the rubber band into a Jacob's ladder, twanging it with my thumbs.

"I like the way it smells before a storm," he says. "I like the way it rains real hard."

"In February, now, a thunderstorm's unusual, but soon it'll be spring and the earth will wake up again. Oh, Chet, I know what I can bring you! A weather kit, with a wind gauge and a barometer and thermometer and pictures of tornadoes and, oh, all sorts of things. Would you like that, Chet?"

His voice comes out flat, like he's speaking underwater: "Quit fooling with that rubber band. It's making me nervous."

Startled, my hands freeze. Chet turns toward the window with his head cocked, tuned to the piping lure of the other children's voices outside. In another instant he's out the door, hatless, coatless, running to join the others, escaping me, free.

Mrs. Anderson's in the kitchen stirring a crock of pinto beans. It took hundreds of dollars to win her slow trust. She takes in my old jeans, cheap blouse, and widening girth with cruel approval. I see myself through her eyes: no hairstyle, just lumpy curls and limp zigzags of fringe, my hands always up in front of my face; but that's an old person's gesture, isn't it, and I'm not thirty yet. I put my hands in my jeans pockets. Mrs. Anderson carries her bully's weight heavily, proudly. Today she wears a poncho over her shoulders, and earrings that dangle loose beside her greasy bun.

"I got some leftover poinsettias you can have if you want 'em, Nancy," she says. "Get Chet and one of the bigger boys to he'p put 'em in your car. They're out in the new greenhouse."

(Yes, a new greenhouse, with the finest heating system available, installed by the best air-control specialists in Richmond; I gave her the check last year for the down payment, when my nightmares were especially bad.)

"Poinsettias? Thank you. Mrs. Anderson, about tomorrow—could I take Chet to a movie, or to Maymont Park? He was so distracted today, I'm sure he remembers. I talked with his teacher on Wednesday. She said he's been depressed lately. She said, for show and tell, he drew this picture of somebody lying down and he said, 'This is a dead guy, got hit by a car.' We won't go to the movies till after church, of course," I add hastily; tomorrow's Sunday.

"Uh-uh. No movies on Sunday. Besides, it's Chet's turn to read the prayer in morning and evening chapel, both."

I knew she would deny the movie, just as I know she's lying about the prayer. But it's futile to argue, just as it was futile to try and get her to let Chet have a puppy. I wasted all last summer begging to give him a puppy, or at least riding lessons. She said a puppy was too much trouble, and riding lessons would make the others jealous. The implication that I should pay for riding lessons for all nine children was the first implication I have ignored for two years. I can't afford it. Her twin enterprises—greenhouse and foster home—have swallowed up my earnings as a guide in a downtown museum.

She doesn't often let me take him places. On our few excursions Chet sits silent, far over on his side of the car. The worst time was our trip to King's Dominion, when we rode through to look at the wild animals. Screeching baboons sprang onto the car, peeled the chrome strips from its sides, mooned us with their orange behinds through the windshield, pounded on the hood with sticks. I grew hysterical. Chet pulled out his history book and ignored them, but he must have told Mrs. Anderson about the incident, because she hasn't let me take him anywhere since.

"Are you ever going to marry that Roger?" Mrs. Anderson asks. She met Roger, my ex-boyfriend, once when he helped me bring in Chet's Christmas presents.

"Roger and I aren't seeing each other anymore." She has no right to ask me anything, but I haven't the strength to fight her, any more than I had the strength to hold onto Roger, any more than Roger knew how to deal with me after the accident. Her back is to me as she stirs the beans, their waxy odor rising from the pot in puffs of steam. Her sharp shoulder blades speak of triumph for my loss, and disappointment that Roger's checkbook eludes her.

She turns around. "Here, put these in the pans." She hands me cupcake wrappers and muffin tins, and as I separate the gaily colored papers—yellow, pink, blue, and white, crinkled around the edges—the enormity of my guilt sweeps over me, the memory of his blood and the sounds he made there on the road, and the froggy smell that rose up from the ditch on either side of that road, and the grief chokes me again, oh, like thousands of times before, and I hate Mrs. Anderson for exhaling loudly at the sound of my tears. "I can't stand it," I sob. "I wish—I wish—"

"He's dead, and nothing'll bring him back. I've never told you this before," and her eyes drink in my misery, giving back a pinhead's worth of comfort, "but he used to like to eat citronella candles, the kind that keeps the bugs away. He would've died anyway, with all that wax in his stomach, eating them candles like other kids eat licorice sticks."

Rage flashes through me so fast I think I've been sliced in two. "Your mammoth ignorance astounds me. You're not fit to raise anybody. Don't you think these children know you only keep them for the money? For you it was like an ant got run over, never mind that he'd been here since he was only four!"

She snatches the cupcake pan out of my hands. "You're a pain in the ass, you know that? You know what Chet's teacher said to me? She called me up to say, 'That Nancy Meade is nuts, cuckoo, it's nasty the way she hangs around Chet so much, they'll both get sick ideas!' "

Before I can respond, there's a little girl in the doorway; Frances, her name is. I've given her hairbands and coloring books before. She must have heard everything. Now she says, "Chet's lying down in the road and won't get up. They sent me to get you." It's me she's looking at, not Mrs. Anderson. Mutely I follow the child out the door and then we're running across the thin grass, still snow bitten around the edges, to where I see children gathered around a still form. My stomach stings, my head swims, I can't keep up with my own rapid feet.

Chet is sprawled out on the road, his eyes shut and his arms thrown sideways. One of the other boys says, "He won't move. We keep tellin' him a car could come, but he won't get up."

"Chet?" I say. "Chet, please get up. We don't want you to get hurt."

He remains immobile. I kneel down and shake his shoulder. It's happening again; I must have killed him, too, and my heart swells so much I can hardly speak: "Oh Chet, I love you, I love you!" Swift as a serpent, he rears up and hurls a handful of sharp stones right in my face, my eyes. I stumble backward, fighting the pain. I can feel blood oozing down my cheek.

"Get away from me, Nancy Meade! You killed my brother. Don't come back here ever, *ever!*"

I weave back to my car. A rock whizzes past my ear, another slaps the back of my head. As I throw the car into gear and drive dizzily away, Chet chases me, his eyes white, his spigot-like neck stretched out long as he screams, "You're fat and ugly and you've got hairy arms and everybody knows what you did and you oughta die for killing my brother! I hate you, I hate you, I hate your guts!" His voice follows me far down the road.

In my dreams he eats earthworms for protein, so starved in that greenhouse that he digs them out of the dirt and swallows them whole. I've been run over by a truck so that I'm flat in the middle, and it hurts, and I snuffle through my broken teeth for help, but only Chet and Mrs. Anderson come to me. Who else would come? Chet towers over me, his legs an A-frame, laughing and laughing, while Mrs. Anderson bellows like a foghorn.

I try to tell myself You're free, he's just a child and she's a greedy lowdown piece of nothing, they've got nothing on you, it couldn't be helped. Haven't I done all I could? What is this all about? It started with a child named Ronnie. He wouldn't have wanted this for anybody. I am absolutely sure he would have grown up kind and fair and bursting with forgiveness.

To Ashes

The deaf man who lived at the end of the road was the one who smelled the fire first, smelled it even before the warehouse owner did, the owner making love in the back with a thin girl: one eye green, one eye brown. It was hot that fall, a low hazy heat like pain. Sap ran out of the sweet gum trees. The warehouse owner, lying on his cot, felt his skin itching all over, like hunger, or like he was allergic to the dimness in that back room, with its one window still covered with heavy plastic from last winter. The thin girl worked at the post office; her mouth tasted of tape and stamp glue.

The deaf man smelled smoke and came out of his house to see the first few plumes weaving skyward, smoke snakes charmed by music he couldn't hear, the music of fire eating through wood. At first he'd thought it was something burning in his own house. He feared a fire in his house. But it wasn't. He stood on his lawn, swiveling his head this way and that, like an ancient astrologer scanning the quadrants for a favorable sign, and then he saw the smoke paling away from the warehouse.

"Hhh, hmm." He made his sounds of comprehension, smacking his hands together as if they were what carried the message to his brain. Of course he had no telephone (though in stores, and in people's houses, he often picked up telephones because he liked their shape). He ran next door to tell the Correys: Mrs. Correy and her sick son, Marlin, a former champion javelin-thrower, the hope of the local high school until he'd hurt his head in an accident. The deaf man found Mrs. Correy hanging laundry. He approached her from the other side of a sheet she was pinning to the line, and she jumped. As he pointed to the clouds, gesturing and making his small sounds of alarm, sounds like graphs of questions, it occurred to him that perhaps he really was the first and only one to notice the fire. He marveled that the others hadn't smelled the smoke or felt the heat, for he sensed the air warming with impunity, hot breath from an open mouth about to say terrible words. Or like the heat from an iron or a new burn on your skin. When his wife was alive, he always knew when she was ironing, no matter where he was in the house, because he could smell the starch and the pure clean seethe of the iron.

Mrs. Correy dropped her clothespins and ran into the house, crying out for her son. The deaf man stood quite still in her yard, the shirts on the line stretching out their sleeves like tight wings, for now there was a wind. A pair of furry yellow socks dangled, Marlin's socks. Yellow socks like something a butterfly would wear, pollen on its feet. Yet Marlin was a big man and not stupid, even though he'd been hurt.

Marlin and his mother swung out of the house, Marlin holding one hand to his ear and making a dialing motion with his other hand, to tell the deaf man that he'd made the call. Mrs. Correy touched her son's arm, her face radiant, and sprinted toward the fire, her heels pounding into the dust; she turned back to beckon to her son and then hurried on.

Marlin wavered. He and the deaf man gazed transfixed at the darkening, thickening smoke, not yet billows, just scuff marks on the white humid sky. The fire alarm sounded so loudly that the deaf man felt a brick shuttling to and fro in his brain, though he couldn't hear the reeling blast, the stuck-horn sound that made businessmen in their wide ties break into a run on the sidewalks, dash breathlessly into the firehouse and into their protective suits. The town was so small that farmers in their nearby fields responded, too, dropping sacks of chicken feed, tossing shovels to the ground, leaping into pickup trucks or simply running through their rows of cornstalks. The town was so small that from Mrs. Correy's yard the deaf man could see it all: the farmers' fields; the main street where the businessmen worked; the train station, where the train still stopped every other day; his own house and those beyond it; and finally the warehouse, with its nougat-colored walls and the mess of telephone wires around it like guywires. Next to the warehouse lay a field where three horses grazed. It was these horses for whom the deaf man now feared. He loved to watch them canter. Urgently, he turned to Marlin, but Marlin did not know the sign for "horse."

It was October, but it was hot, as if the year had forgotten that fall was due. Perhaps the warehouse fire was simply the long Alabama summer, burning at last. It had been a season so dry that the deaf man often found small birds dead of thirst in a garden too parched for flowers to bloom. He himself worked several days a week in the warehouse, stacking boxes on the early shift, and then he returned home and ate supper in his hot kitchen, where a line of ants marched across the formica countertop, a line of mean little biting ants that made him nervous because he didn't know where they came from and couldn't make them go away. New ones appeared to take the places of the ones he killed.

Marlin's mouth was moving; the deaf man looked up and saw flames. They moved toward the warehouse slowly at first, and then they were running.

"Jesus, Bernard, I've got to get my pocketbook!" The girl was coughing. Because the dank back room had no outside door, the girl and the warehouse owner had to take the long corridor to escape outside. But halfway down the long hallway, the girl paused, irresolute. "I left my pocketbook in your office!"

The man put his hand on the back of her neck. "Get down as close as you can to the floor and breathe the air down there. Forget about your pocketbook. Stay close behind me."

She obeyed because it was natural to her to obey him. Lovers since June, they'd been meeting each afternoon, after she closed up the post office. She knew Bernard didn't love her, and she knew he was married, but she couldn't give him up. She knew her looks didn't please many men. Her bony fingers, her slack body. He teased her about her mismatched eyes. She thought about him all the time. But still they were connected to the world in separate ways. It was she who had smelled the smoke first, waking him on the narrow cot.

Now the smoke thickened, and it was not black or gray but a pale color, like the skin on the parts of the body that never see the sun. The deaf man, standing just inside the chain-link fence surrounding the warehouse yard, peered through the crowd, spotted Mrs. Correy, and thought how ugly she was. He didn't reproach himself for the thought; he simply marveled at how people thought awful things about each other all the time yet still managed to get along. He would never tell Mrs. Correy how ugly he thought she was. Maybe she thought he was ugly, too. But they would go on waving and smiling forever, and there she was now, in the midst of the throng gathered round the warehouse, a throng expressing what the deaf man thought of as fire emotion: yelling, craning their heads, running about, standing on tiptoe and bending low. Were there still people in the building?

Workers in smocks ran out like loose grapes, some carrying parcels that they had been moving or stacking, others clutching lunchboxes or purses. The deaf man knew about Kitty and Bernard, because every weekday he watched Kitty lock up the post office and walk over to the warehouse, ducking her head as she entered. He knew about them as surely as if it had been written in the paper. He looked for them now, but he didn't see them.

People pushed all around him, and he realized that one's clothes could get wrinkled in a crowd, simply from bodies rubbing up against each other.

But where was Marlin? The deaf man looked about, and then he saw Marlin's back disappearing into the melee, his big shoulders knotted as if to throw a javelin. The deaf man had seen that strength five years before, when Marlin set the high school record for distance throwing. And once, the deaf man and Marlin had pushed a stranger's car to the filling station because the car was out of gas. Now Marlin headed into the warehouse with that pushing-a-car look on his back.

Marlin was thinking of Bernard, who was a friend of his late father's. But even more, he was thinking of Kitty. He thought about her a lot. At night, when the motion of the train on the rails made his bed shake, he thought of her. He knew she lived in a little apartment over the post office; he'd seen her taking down her flowered curtains from the second-story window, perhaps to wash them, and then putting them back up. He had seen her slip into the warehouse, and his feelings for her had sprung up like mushrooms after rain, so that he bought stamps more often than necessary.

Now, swooping into hallways solid with smoke, the idea of rescue made him brave, and he was sick with wanting her. In high school, girls wanted him, and he had them beneath the bleachers, in the dark. But after he hurt his head while working on his car— a stupid accident, the hood of the car fell down and knocked him out, nothing of mystery or heroism in it—he almost died, and now, though he was as strong as ever, he couldn't concentrate on things for very long, so he couldn't keep a job, and women seemed to forget he was a man, except when there was work to be done.

There they were, on the floor: Bernard and Kitty. Alive? Marlin's lungs burned in his chest as he tried to lift them both, but Bernard was so heavy. Marlin tried again. He slung Kitty over his shoulder and rolled Bernard into his outstretched arms. But when he stood up, he staggered.

Outside, the deaf man chewed his thumbnail as the fire gave off a crisp smell like clean paper scorching. He was afraid Marlin would become disoriented in the building, would forget where he was. The deaf man forgot all about the horses that he loved, the horses bucking in their paddock beside the warehouse yard, and he smacked his temples with his knuckles in an effort to think better.

Then the windows of the building went navy blue. It was frightful, yet it was grand, something new, like drinking from an underground stream, and the deaf man forgot about his fear for Marlin in the headlong rush of the scene: the firefighters leaping off their trucks, the great hoses looping forward, catching for a maddening instant on a dead tree limb, a child clinging to the deaf man's knees in a sudden inexplicable cleaving. He saw fear on Mrs. Correy's face, and he felt a sudden evil delight that she was threatened; then he shook the badness away from him. Mrs. Correy flapped her apron as if to fan the flames.

Suddenly the crowd pulsed, and the deaf man felt the humming along his nerves that meant a great cry was going up. There was Marlin, strong like a living statue, striding out of the hell with Kitty limp in his arms. Behind him, the navy blue windows popped. The ground shook, the horses screamed, a wall of fire crested over the roof, and a terrible trampling began as people brutally, hysterically, kicked and elbowed their way through the mob, shrieking and fighting. Cinders rained, and, though he didn't know it, the deaf man was screaming too.

It burned all night. But still, morning came. The big wreck smoldered just like the firemen said it would, and that day and in the following days, people from other towns came to look at it, while the horses in the paddock chewed grass, oblivious. The farmers said some of their stock died of fright. Hens stopped laying for a while. The warehouse workers jerked their smocks over their heads in the morning, until they remembered that they had no workplace to go to. But still, morning came, and other mornings.

It grew cold, and by the time the trees reddened at last, children played in the wreck, hoping to find live coals beneath the fallen timbers.

Kitty left. Another woman took her place at the post office, and Marlin moped around his house and his yard, shooing his mother away or cursing her sharply, like he never used to do. Sometimes he cried, pantomiming to the deaf man: "I left him there. It's all my fault." Winter came, and then spring, a cold spring with a mean wind that ripped the heads off the tulips. There was a change in the deaf man's heart, a change that had to do with Marlin. He grew tired of Marlin always sobbing and shaking, always coming over and doing nothing in particular, just bending over and picking up sticks, his face red and staring, his burnt arm bandaged long after the need for bandages was over, talking wildly about what he should have done. One day, exasperated, the deaf man drew an ugly picture on a piece of paper and pointed to Marlin's mother, and Marlin shook like a big machine coming apart, his bottom teeth showing. The deaf man crumpled the picture, shut his eyes, prayed, What have I done? He knew he had seen something dreadful, had seen the last purposeful move a man would make.

The deaf man's house was at the end of the road. Beyond it lay a field where crows circled. The deaf man didn't try to analyze the pull of Marlin to Kitty, because that was what it was to love. What did bother him was Marlin's guilt, guilt born of hatred at a time when there was no time to think, so that Bernard was left on the floor and Kitty was saved. Her curtains sagged in the empty apartment over the post office.

It was April. Marlin shambled about the yard, pointing at the crows, churning the rusty pump handle up and down, waving his arms in anger when his mother called, throwing a stick as if it were a javelin or a pencil. He was crying, and when he cried he was ugly. None of the athlete's grace remained. He was old, and he was not yet twenty-four.

The deaf man had done without speech for a long time, but now he wanted loud words to send Marlin away. What made Marlin bad, like the fire? Sometimes, from inside the house, the deaf man laughed at him.

Marlin was at the pump, jerking the handle like a living thing he wanted to hurt. I have to help him, the deaf man thought. He crossed the yard to stand in front of Marlin and placed his hand on Marlin's cheek. The stubble of beard shocked him—the vitality of it—and he drew his hand away, confronted by the physical reality of the man's sad red eyes, his sweat smell, the warmth of that cheek. Where to begin? If only he could tell him: Marlin, you must practice standing still.

Squabs

Mr. Moses was short, fat, bald, excitable. He wore baggy suits, round spectacles, and a watch-chain (even eight-year-old Billie knew watch-chains weren't worn anymore), and he drove an old yellow Cadillac. He rented the old stucco hip-roofed barn from Billie's father, and in it he stored the parts of an enormous pipe organ.

Billie had watched the pipes being stacked inside, and she tried hard to imagine how the organ would look put together, how it would sound. Mr. Moses said it had belonged to a big Baptist church up in Raleigh, and when the church was torn down, he'd bought the organ because he loved the way hymns sounded on it. Mr. Moses came by the house on the first of each month to pay the rent, and every six months or so he stayed all afternoon to tune the piano at which Billie practiced, reluctantly, when she came home from school. Once he arrived at eleven o'clock at night, clutching two gallons of French vanilla ice cream, which Billie was allowed to stay up and eat even though the hour was late, because her parents could rarely afford to buy ice cream.

In the two years that Mr. Moses had been using it, the barn had become infested with pigeons. At first there were only two or three cooing on the roof, but then suddenly there were dozens, rustling and startling one another and making sounds that were not songs but rhythmic ruminating noises in a kind of chorus. Billie feared their gimlet eyes. They watched her swinging on the long rope hung from a backyard elm, and Billie waved her arms at

them and yelled. She, who loved animals, who watched over the
dozen cats her family owned, found no love in her heart for the
pigeons, only a certain fascination in the birds' power to upset Mr.
Moses. They were nesting in his beloved pipes.

First Mr. Moses tried mothballs. He sputtered and raged about
the expense, the time, the inconvenience, about the way mothballs
gave him headaches. Billie watched as he entered the barn with a
naptha-laden sack, his suit draped with a sheet. An hour later he
emerged with an empty sack and an angry smile. But the mothballs didn't work; the birds simply grew hardier and more numer-
ous than ever.

So he attempted to smoke them out. Billie and her mother arrived home from the grocery store one day to find Mr. Moses setting fire to several large barrels of pitch. He coughed, waving oily
black smoke away from his face, while Billie's mother frantically
predicted that he'd not only lose his lease but also burn the barn
down. She begged him to take the barrels away before her husband
came home. Muttering, he did so.

The struggle between Mr. Moses and the birds was becoming
something of a joke in the community. Billie was learning, first
slowly and painfully, then with a growing burden of pride, that her
family—and, by extension, Mr. Moses—were regarded as eccen-
tric by many of their neighbors. She knew, from the whispering
tongues at the grocery store, on the playground, on the shaded
porches where she and her mother sometimes visited, that the
townspeople thought her mother was high-handed and her father a
wild man, and she a strange little creature who did well in school
and didn't like to play with the other children. Only the butcher at
the grocery store was kind, saving bushels of fish heads each Fri-
day to give to Billie's mother, who carried them proudly out of the
store. Billie hated the way the fish heads smelled, but she loved
the task of feeding the cats, dumping the basket out on a far corner of a field, near the woods. Her whip-thin cats swarmed round
her ankles and snatched at the gleaming gilled heads.

She heard the swift tongues clattering about the house, the cats,
the fish heads, and her frayed dresses, but she didn't question the
way her family lived. She believed in her parents' business sense.

After all, weren't they in charge of the rent for the barn? And wasn't there always enough money for her weekly piano lessons, even though Billie would gladly have sacrificed that particular luxury?

But there was something else that fall, sly voices saying that her mother had been seen with a man who kept a motel out on the highway, a man whom Billie had never seen but whose name she grew to fear, flinching if she heard it in casual conversation between adults at school or at the store, adults who then looked at her with wide eyes.

Billie's mother kept close to the house, doing her chores. She had a habit of twisting her long braided hair in her hands, a habit that Billie thought looked unhappy. The rumormongering voices also spoke about Billie's piano teacher, the too-tall, too-thin, goateed piano teacher, and Billie's mother's black eyes grew cold. Then it was only the name of the motelkeeper again. Sometimes Billie thought she heard his name in the roosting coos of the pigeons up in the barn loft, the pigeons that continued to defy the furious denunciations of Mr. Moses.

One November afternoon Billie's father came home with his face white and his fists clenched. He and Billie's mother locked themselves in their room, while Billie slunk around the door with her face like ice. She heard her father ask her mother about the rumors, and she heard her mother say No, no, no, and after a while there was silence, until her father burst out of the room, stomped outside, and began to work on one of his amateur racing cars. Billie's mother stayed behind the closed door.

It was so warm outside that it felt more like summer than fall. Billie didn't need a sweater, and she walked barefoot into the driveway, her toughened soles impervious to the small stones and broken tar. Her father assaulted the engine of a rusty car. Billie could tell he didn't even know she was there, but she preferred to be outside with him just then, rather than inside with her mother. She stared at his sharp-nosed profile and his freckled, oil-smudged cheek. She'd noticed the way people gazed at her parents when they were out together; she could tell there was something striking in her father's fierce face and in her mother's small proud figure,

something about the way they looked together. Suddenly her father
looked very young to her. She thought of how he, too, got cold in
the drafty house and ate the meals that were mostly bread, to
make the meat go farther. He, too, must have heard the pigeons
cooing. He must have heard people's cruel voices rippling behind
him as he walked around the town.

Just then Mr. Moses' old yellow Cadillac turned into the driveway and rolled toward them. Briefly, Mr. Moses spoke to Billie
and her father and then stumped off toward the barn. Billie ran
after him, sensing something, climbed the knotted rope swing, and
waited.

A row of gray pigeons rocked in the open loft. Far off, crows
wavered in the pines, and near Billie a redwing blackbird swooped
to the top of the elm from which the swing dangled. The pigeons
weren't like the crows or the blackbirds, Billie knew; their eyes
were different, as was the way they established their nests so
openly in a building instead of nesting hidden in the tops of trees.

Mr. Moses disappeared into the barn, and after a moment Billie
heard him yelling. The cries echoed within the barn and back in
the pine woods, and Billie felt afraid. Her father heard Mr. Moses
and came running, and then Mr. Moses burst out of the barn with
hundreds of tiny soft feathers clinging to his bald head and to his
clothes, and with cobwebs on his suit and his hands. He stormed
toward her father, and in the tirade that followed, Billie learned
that the young had hatched. There'd be more birds.

"You've got to help me!" cried Mr. Moses. "Got to get rid of
them or I'll take my pipes out, and you need that rent—"

Billie's father swore, then bellowed over Mr. Moses' voice.
"We'll finish this thing! I'm sick of your complaining!" He spun
and dashed away from Mr. Moses and Billie, leaving them staring
at each other. A light breeze lifted a few feathers from Mr. Moses'
shoulders. As Billie clung to the thick hemp of her swing, a picture formed in her mind: the vision of a thousand brass pipes
blasting songs and birds skyward.

"What's he gonna do?" Mr. Moses asked her softly, but before
she could answer, her father charged out of the house with his
long, dark shotgun in his arms. Her mother ran after him, the cats

scattering and hissing on the porch as she tumbled out of the screen door, screaming at him to stop, to give the gun to her, that she wasn't worth it, that the motelkeeper wasn't worth it, that nothing like that was worth killing for. She clung to his arm, but he shook her away and reeled down the porch steps toward the barn. Billie's mother followed him, crying, her old dress catching the wind.

Billie's toes dug the earth beneath her swing. As her father approached, Mr. Moses raised his arms in surrender, his whole body shaking, and he murmured, "Please, please don't kill me! I won't say any more about the birds." Billie's father lifted the gun to the sky and fired. The birds in the rafters flew out of the loft and sailed dizzily away from the barn, and he shot them. Ten, eleven, twelve fell to the ground, and a black cat streaked out from the edge of the woods to retrieve a limp feathered body. At another report from the gun, a second flock flew out above the red roof, and the air cracked again. More bodies plummeted, and another cat, belly low to the grass, darted forward to clasp a bird in its jaws.

Billie's mother was crying. Billie's father stood there with his body taut as a hunter's, the rifle like part of his arm. There were live birds spinning in the gray sky and shattered birds all over the ground, and Mr. Moses was still holding his hands above his head as if he'd forgotten they were there. Billie thought, It's over, it's over. Billie's father pumped shots into the air so rapidly that the blasts and the echoes were all they could hear, shots fused into a single explosion in their four separate brains.

Smoketown Road

Irene Sterling stood in the Methodist church singing "Fairest Lord Jesus," her frayed yellow hair rising and falling as she fanned herself. She heard her cow, Pet, mooing from down the road, and she realized: Pet sounds different to me than to anybody else in this church, just because she's mine. Across the pew, old Dave Dixon tried to wink at her, but he couldn't wink very well and it was just a hard blink. As the song ended, Dave Dixon stage-whispered, "Moo! Moo!" and she smiled with her eyes half-closed.

It was July, eleven-thirty-two in the morning. The church still held a faint protective coolness, though hot sunlight arched through the windows. Honeysuckle snaked across the screens, the tendrils reminding Irene of her baby's hair. She'd left the baby home with Gunther, her husband.

The church was little, but it had the highest ceiling Irene had ever seen. Thorny metal lights swung from that ceiling, each light layered with dead flies. How old could the oldest fly-body be in those lights—twenty, fifty years old? The church was built long ago. They didn't have electric lights back then, but flies would have looked exactly the same, and honeysuckle smelled the same, and people's voices sounded the same, even these very hymns, and there were times, like now, when people just sat and thought and waited for whatever was next.

Gunther came to church with her sometimes, but he'd rather stay home with the baby, work on his carpentry, watch TV. He claimed that when he heard the singing, he could tell Irene's voice apart from the others. She didn't think this could be true, but it pleased her. He went to church on Monday nights, but then it wasn't for church; it was for the alcoholic meetings. It was comforting to look across the road and see the diamond-shaped church lights burning yellow in the darkness.

She counted: twenty-six people here today, including the preacher. Not bad. Smoketown wasn't a town, just a place. Apart from a few farms, a post office, the rival church (Baptist), and a general store, the area was as green and blank as a county map. Red and green, red because of the Georgia clay. Livestock grew well and sometimes corn, but the cornworms got so bad they could make you cry. Most of the farmers had long ago switched to beans. Gunther said, "This land is beautiful, but it's not good."

Twenty-six people, but then, that was because the Addison family had their daughter and her husband visiting, and all five McTeagues were there, which was rare. There was no Sunday School, because there weren't enough children to have it. But Gunther was always talking about how the county was changing, with new people moving in, a steady influx of strangers streaming down Smoketown Road, buying up the farms. "There's that hotshot foot doctor with his Cuban wife," he'd say, "not that I have anything against Cubans, and there's those weirdos that do weaving, who bought the old Kincaid place, and those Norwegians who want to start a symphony here. More power to 'em. I'll pitch in and play my comb."

Gunther wasn't an alcoholic, but he went to the meetings anyway. "To help 'em," he said. He liked to know about people. But he himself was part flesh and part smoke: he told Irene that he'd had an identity change, that the government had decided his name would be Gunther Sterling, with such-and-such a Social Security number, and he could be the same person on the inside that he'd always been, but to the world he would be a new person. When she asked what he'd done before, he got wild, talking about working for the White House. When she asked where he was from, he first said Oregon, then West Virginia.

"Well, I never met a West Virginian I didn't like," she said, because one of her old boyfriends was from West Virginia. Gunther thought that was cute, and he made the phrase his own.

"What if I went all through the alphabet, through all the names there are, trying to guess your real name?" she asked him once.

"I'm trained," he said, "trained to forget that old name and not jump at the sound of it, even if somebody whispers it in the dark, or screams it at my back in a public place."

When they got married, she didn't love him. She married him because she was twenty-eight and tired of waiting, tired of still living with her parents, who had itchy feet to retire and move away. When Gunther came strolling down Smoketown Road with nothing to his name but his set of carpentry tools, his voice loud as a flag clanging on a flagpole on a windy day, she said yes to him, quick as a heartbeat. He said, "All you need to know about me is I'm the kind of man will stay up all night to kill a damn buzzing fly."

She never knew what he had done before. He was her husband, a lot older than she was, with white creeping into his rumpled hair, the hair that reminded her of cornstalks smashed by hail. At first she asked a lot of questions—did he have anything to do with bombs or war or Russians?—and he said he'd told her too much already. They were happy together. He built their house himself, right next to the river, which ran fast and muddy and wide. They had a view of the Double Mountains to the east, not mountains, just hills, gently peaked, "like the breasts of some huge lady stretched out on the land," said Gunther.

The government even gave him a different birthday. She watched him on other days to see if he was acting like it was a secret birthday, his old birthday, but he never let on.

The preacher was talking about yard sales. "We always want something for a bargain price," he said. This was a new young preacher who drove all the way from Dalton because they couldn't find anybody around here. He was nervous and sweaty, and the preacher-gown didn't fit right, because he was every bit as fat as the Talleys, who ran the general store and sold things for ridiculous prices, prices so high nobody ever went there unless they were desperate. Once, when Irene and Gunther both had the flu and were too sick to drive to the Safeway, twenty minutes away by car, she'd gone to that Talley store and paid so much for a can of tuna and a box of ice cream that it still made her mad, just to remember.

"Think how happy you'd be if you stumbled onto some precious jewels at a yard sale," said the preacher, and Irene pictured card tables set up on a lawn, dotted with diamonds. Her wedding ring was from J. C. Penney, gold and pretty. Gunther'd picked it out. "But anything really valuable like that, you probably wouldn't find at a yard sale, now, would you?" The preacher mopped his face. Behind him Sallie, the organist, checked her lipstick in the little mirror above her sheet music. Irene had seen Sallie check that mirror, kissing the air, as often as ten times during a service.

"The best things just find you, instead of you finding them. It's like taking in a stray animal," said the preacher, his palms up. Irene linked yard sales and stray animals in her mind; it made sense. "My wife and I do that, take in strays," the preacher concluded, and motioned for Sallie to play the next hymn.

There's a nail in my thoughts, Irene admitted to herself, in the middle of "O for a Thousand Tongues to Sing." Something was bothering her, something that her thoughts kept catching on, like a nylon stocking might catch on a splinter. Her mother used to say: There's a nail in my thoughts, and I'd give anything for the hammer that'd pry it out. But now her mother was gone, and her father too, moved to Mexico of all places. They'd never even seen Mexico before, but when they got old, they sold their farm and left Georgia and lit out for Guadalajara, saying how cheap you could live down there, and though they wrote, "Come see us and bring the baby," Irene felt that she was an identity they had left behind. She was to them what Gunther's old Social Security number was to him. Anyway, she couldn't afford to get to Mexico, and something was wrong with the baby.

If she said it, then it would be true. But not saying it was starting to hurt. The doctor hadn't seemed to notice, but of course he was so busy, all he did was give the baby her shots. Nurses chirped, "Isn't she cute?" but Irene knew only she and Gunther really thought so. The baby was slow to react to things, even when you waved your fingers in front of her face or put her own hand right on Pet, the cow. The baby was the color of home-canned peaches, and she was soft and never said a word. Her name was Melody. Her lips and eyelids were thick, and she was so quiet, sometimes Irene forgot she was in the room. Now she was three. Irene had heard the word "slow" used to describe some people. People treated slow people funny. She remembered a slow boy in her elementary school, who left after the second grade and just stayed home with his mother.

For that matter, people treated Gunther funny. Nobody could call him slow, but they thought he was crazy. One Monday night the alcoholics threw him out of the meeting, accusing him of spying. But he insisted he used to drink, long ago, and now was reformed, so they let him come back. The thing was, he told everybody about the identity change, so people actually asked Irene about it. She'd just say, "If it isn't true, it makes a mighty good story."

Gunther wasn't young anymore. Maybe that had something to do with the baby being the way she was. But Gunther was healthy, and he wasn't old, and Irene was only thirty-four. Sometimes people took Gunther for Melody's grandfather, but it didn't bother Gunther or Irene, either one.

Dave Dixon nudged her. "You're gonna miss the fried chicken," he said, and she realized church was over, the pews were suddenly empty. It was Picnic Sunday, and the women were already out on the lawn, unpacking hampers of fried chicken, slaw, potato chips, cupcakes.

"I'll go get Gunther," she said. She had forgotten about the picnic. Passing through the small, musty church foyer, she shook hands with the preacher. It was like squeezing raw hamburger.

"I like yard sales, too," she said. She doubted she would ever see him again. Preachers came once or twice and then never again, because there wasn't much money here, or much of a way to get known, in whatever way preachers tried to get known.

To the women who called out to her on the lawn she said, "I'm going home to fetch Gunther and Melody, and I'll be right back," and then she crossed the road. But instead of going straight home she turned left and walked down to the bridge. Below her the river rushed by, reddish and high from last week's rain.

Once, four summers ago, there'd been a dead pony caught on the rocks in the middle of the river, a pitiful sight even though it was already dead. It was Gunther who pulled it out with a rope and hauled it away in his truck. By then they'd been married two years, but that was the day she fell in love with him, seeing how strong he was. Her indifference melted away, like chocolate coating melting off a cookie, and ever since then she'd loved him.

She walked down to the water's edge, careless of her white vinyl sandals. The river smelled ripe and earthy, and the breeze cooled her skin. What if Gunther was crazy? What if she found his old high school yearbook, with a young picture of him in it and the name "Gunther Sterling" at the bottom? Then she'd know for sure that all those stories were just tall tales. She plucked a fistful of trumpetvine and jewelweed from the riverbank and made her way back to the house.

She went inside. Gunther was standing at the living room window with a pair of binoculars in his hand and the baby crouching at his feet. Gunther squinted through the binoculars and said, "Oh, no. Grace McTeague brought the green stuff again, that green dip that everybody hated last year. Her husband's got irons in the fire, did I tell you? Monday night, he talked a blue streak about a puppet theater he's planning with the Norwegians."

"Gunther," Irene began. She went and stood beside him, picking Melody up in her arms. "We've got to talk about Melody. Something's not right. All through church, I thought about her."

He put the binoculars down. "I know," he said quietly. "I wonder what to do when you can't go forward and can't go back. I got a new start, but I can't do that for her, and maybe nobody can, and I don't know what to do."

Outside, Pet mooed; the picnickers' merriment drifted across the road. Gunther took the baby from Irene and held the binoculars to Melody's small face, but the baby just turned her head away. Gently, Gunther set Melody down on the sofa.

To Irene's surprise, there were tears in Gunther's eyes. She realized she didn't care if his stories were lies, every one of them. She said, "What will happen to Melody, when we die?"

"We've got a long while yet. We'll think of something." He reached out, took a sprig of jewelweed from Irene's hand, and tucked it into her long hair.

"Want to go to that picnic?" she said. But he just held her, and she held him.

A Neighborhood Story

Mignon Kruse has a crazy child—an honest-to-goodness insane six-year-old that she keeps penned up in her yard. Mignon herself is a puzzle—the things she says take me all day to figure out, when I have the time to think about them. "I don't regret anything I've ever done in my life," she said, when I bought a Bible from her, "but there are a lot of things I'd do differently, if I could." Her child's name is Knox. I'm Patrice. Knox really is crazy, but I can't feel sorry for him, because I don't like him. When Mignon brings him over, he says things like, "I don't want to eat anything off a tray." Mignon lets him wear his hair in one of those tails at the back of the neck, which I don't approve of.

This morning Knox bit the mailman. The mailman wears his khaki shorts so well that he looks like he's on safari. His long wiry hair fans out in the breeze. I saw him find a pair of sunglasses one day, good ones just lying on the sidewalk, and I wished I'd found them first. I dream about finding things, mostly money. This mailman has to walk through rain sometimes, but never snow; it's warm in this part of Virginia, except when February sharpens its teeth on your cold, raw wrists. We've always got clouds in our sky, as if God is smoking.

Anyway, this morning the mailman left a free sample of fabric softener in my mailbox. I never use the stuff, so I plucked it out of the box and started over to give it to Mignon. Lo and behold, Knox came darting out from behind a pyracantha bush and seized the mailman's leg. The man cried out in pain, swatting Knox, and I had to wrestle Knox off the targeted leg. The mailman had the expression people get just before they sneeze. Knox lunged out of my arms and tried to bite him again, but the mailman kicked at him with the toe of his desert boot, so Knox rolled away under the mock orange hedge, where he lay hunched over, heaving. I didn't care about him. If Mignon spanked him more, maybe he wouldn't be crazy. But he really is crazy, she insists; that's why she takes him to a counselor twice a week. Maybe he simply acts out what she herself would like to do: bite the mailman's leg. Where was she, anyway? Nowhere around that I could see.

As the mailman handed me more fabric softener by way of thanks, I knew what I wanted: I wanted somebody who'd make me laugh and cry. I wanted people to drop in on me uninvited. I wanted to live without a telephone. I wanted to go out with the mailman. So I asked him, and he accepted.

The waitress clucks over my fortune cookie: I have left the little white slip on top of my empty dish of green-tea ice cream. It says, Once you commit a sin twice, it no longer seems a sin.

"That's just good advice," the waitress says.

"Not that I'm thinking of sinning," I say. What I am thinking of these days is revenge. Maybe it has something to do with the lack of ventilation in my townhouse, but I'm electrified lately, thinking of all the people I'd like to "get." Of course I can't say this to the mailman, who is seated across from me, rolling his chopsticks between his flat palms.

I'm in trouble: I can't remember what he said his name is. We introduced ourselves so briefly. Did he say John or Jim? Since I can't remember, I don't call him anything. He has the advantage, having seen my name on so many envelopes. If only I could see him write his name down. If he never calls me and thus never has to identify himself over the phone, will I ever find out? What is the longest anybody has ever dated somebody without knowing their name? Are there any married people who don't know each other's names?

"What are you thinking about?" he says.

"What does your mother do?" This is truly important, because my last date, which was a year ago, was with somebody whose mother turned out to be a fortune teller. When I drove over to my date's house to pick him up, there was his mother, wearing a polyester turban and reading somebody's palm in the kitchen, with a pink light on. I felt humiliated for months, though it's hard to say why.

"My mother's a paperboy," he says, grinning. "She delivers newspapers in the most rural county of the state."

"I'm a nurse," I volunteer, because he hasn't asked yet, or does he already know? "Living so close to the hospital, I know whenever something really bad has happened when I'm off duty, because I can hear the helicopters flying overhead. The hospital has a special landing pad on the roof for emergencies."

My boss is one person I'd like to get, my boss with the vacant expression and hair like ground beef; he's mean. I ask the mailman, "If you could shoot five individuals, who would they be? Maybe we know some people in common."

"Besides Mrs. Kruse and her kid, nobody really, except one or two people from a long time ago. Is this something you think about a lot?"

One or two people from a long time ago. How long does it take to get to know somebody? Longer than it used to, is all I know. I'm almost forty; he must be a little younger. That's a lot of time to fill in.

"Mrs. Kruse is in bad shape. She's worse off than her son," he says.

I look down at my empty ice cream dish. I was married for a while, but my husband left me. He was a lot younger. We met at an auction, and he asked me why was I there, to buy dead people's clothes or old rugs? I'd ridden a bus to the auction; he drove me home in his car, but we ran into a storm. It started raining, then flash-flooding, so we pulled over to a roadside bar, drank beer, played pinball, and fell in love. His dark hair flopped over onto his flat cheeks; his gasflame eyes never wavered. We were together for a year, and then he left a note on the refrigerator to say goodbye. I don't tell the mailman any of this.

"You must know a lot about people, from the letters they get," I say. "You know how many bills they have to pay, and how popular they are, and how close their family is. Don't you?"

He's laughing now, his arm thrown over the back of his chair. "For them, I'm just an event in their day—something that makes them mad if it doesn't happen."

The restaurant is closing. The mailman gestures to the bits of trash that a boy is sweeping into a dustpan. "If you sifted through that, Patrice, could you say what these restaurant folks are like?"

I nod, but I'm thinking about what Mignon will say when I tell her about this date. She'll say, "Really, Patrice! The *mailman!*" and somehow, in her world, she'll believe that he was the one who did the biting, not Knox.

The waitress brings the check, and on the credit card slip he signs James. So.

Outside, it's dark and hot. We move down the sidewalk in silence, with enough space between us for an extra person. For a moment I can't remember where I am, who I'm with. Lately I've had these dreams about hawks and eagles and songbirds—fun, but they make nothing clear.

The mailman's face looks pasty under the streetlights. I live just a few blocks from the restaurant where we ate, yet it seems years since I saw my house. It hasn't rained for weeks. Waist-high clouds of dust hang over the street. The houses raise their eyebrows; Knox howls from somewhere in the darkness.

Here we are, at the door. Inside. In my living room it's too hot to turn on the lights, and I'm groping for the electric fan when we hear a helicopter whir by, low, and then another and another. I'm alarmed: "What could've happened?"

The mailman, peering out the window, says, "Police. It's just one copter, with a searchlight on."

"Who're they looking for?" The light pierces the dim square of my patio, the propeller sounding so loud we can't talk. If I were the one the police were looking for, I know what I would do—run to the woods, cover my back with leaves, and lie so still they'd never find me.

"Scary," says the mailman, close to my ear.

Yes, but this is how progress is made. We lean on the sill, looking out, the searchlight scanning our fingers.

Under Glass

All year she'd waited for Christmas, and now it was here, the day spinning by as fast and bright as a dream. She was Fay Williams, a twenty-five-year-old teacher at a Philadelphia prep school, home for Christmas with her family, in Virginia. She sat in the living room holding last year's Christmas snapshots. I'm getting funnier looking every year, she thought, my nose and face are getting longer. She stood up and laid the pictures on the mantelpiece.

Her elbow brushed the Christmas tree, sending an old Santa ornament smashing to the floor.

"Oh, Fay!" sighed her sister Natalie. Natalie had barely spoken all day. It was the first time Fay had seen her since Natalie's wedding three months earlier. Now Natalie and her husband, Evan, lived in the Midwest. Evan had stated repeatedly how long the trip was to Virginia, how many hours they had had to drive.

Her face hot, Fay picked up the broken ornament and threw it away. She was thirsty. "Who'd like some cranberry juice?" she asked. It was her teacher-voice: cheerful, lilting, the enunciation exaggerated.

Natalie didn't respond, but Evan jerked his chin at Fay. Mrs. Coover, a visiting neighbor, nodded. Fay's mother and father smiled distractedly as they talked with two Chinese professors who were visiting under an exchange program. Like Fay's father, the Chinese people taught geology. There was a man, Hoon, and a woman, J.J. They sat side by side on the sofa, their skins the color of eggnog in the cold light pouring in through the window. Fay

liked them; in this moment, because they looked up at her so trust-
ingly, politely, she loved them. Yes, they would like cranberry
juice, too.

In the kitchen she splashed the vivid juice into the good glasses.
Only a little was left in the big bottle, so she held it to her lips and
drank.

"Cranberry juice is good for the bladder," said Mrs. Coover,
who had followed her into the kitchen. "Did your mother make
that jumper?"

"Yes, she did. It matches my blouse, my scarf, even my
socks." She pointed. Still the teacher.

"Your sister's husband's kind of quiet, isn't he? And his last
name is funny; I still can't catch it."

Fay chuckled, because she had known Mrs. Coover would say
that. She sliced some cheese and summer sausage onto a tray and
asked Mrs. Coover, "Would you take this in, please?" as she put
the glasses of cranberry juice on another tray.

Back in the living room, Fay sat on the floor—there were no
more chairs—letting the full skirt of the new jumper billow over
her knees. Someone touched her shoulder: J.J., the Chinese
woman.

"Look, Fay, it's snowing," she said.

Fay turned and peered out the window. The snowflakes whirled
against the pane.

"We must take the flag down!" Fay's father cried. But no one
moved.

"What is this the year of?" Fay asked J.J. "Which animal?"

Hoon answered, "Year of the tiger. That's usually a good year."

"We need a good year," said Fay's mother. She waved a hand
toward Hoon and J.J. and said to Mrs. Coover, "Hey. See if you
can guess their ages."

Fay grimaced, wishing her mother wouldn't.

Mrs. Coover squinted and tilted her head. J.J. and Hoon looked
at Fay. "I'd say . . . twenty-six and forty."

"Wrong!" said Fay's mother, chuckling. "Nobody's guessed
right yet. She's thirty-three and he's thirty-eight."

"I'm tall for a Chinese woman," said J.J. apologetically. As if height corresponded with age, Fay's mind fumbled. "My two brothers, back home, are invited to parties all over Taiwan because they are both six feet tall."

Natalie and Evan rose simultaneously. Natalie touched her husband's hip. "We'll go get the flag, Dad," she said.

Mrs. Coover stirred restlessly. "Can I have the tour now?" she asked Fay's mother. "I want to see the redecorating upstairs."

"I'm resting my bum knee," said Fay's mother. "Fay, you take her upstairs."

As they climbed the stairs, Mrs. Coover gazed right and left. Her voice reached Fay's ear as Fay strode ahead of her: "I heard from Sonny."

Sonny was Mrs. Coover's adopted son. Fay disliked Mrs. Coover intensely, but she had loved Sonny for years, even though she hadn't seen him since they were both seventeen, the year he ran away from home. She remembered her joy when he had escaped from Mrs. Coover's domination. For a long time he had sent Fay postcards from wherever he was living, but that had stopped when she graduated from college.

"And how is Sonny? I never hear from him anymore."

"He got some girl in trouble. They're getting married. It seems awfully old fashioned, don't you think?"

In her sudden rage, Fay wanted to knock Mrs. Coover down the steps. Don't think about Sonny, she told herself. On the landing, she turned, with the professional smile she used for her ninth-graders to ease the news of a pop quiz. "Look at this hallway. Mom's real proud of the way she did it over."

"Sonny said he was up near Philadelphia one weekend last year. Said he tried to call you."

"I usually go to New York on weekends. I have a whole network of friends there." It was the first time Fay had used the word "network" in this way. And she had only two friends in New York.

"Aren't you the least bit curious about Sonny? Heaven knows, *I'm* curious. He hardly tells me anything, and now this."

"Is there more to know?"

Mrs. Coover said triumphantly, "He's not very happy about his marriage, but he's doing what he feels he should."

"Mrs. Coover," Fay took both the woman's hands in her own, "my therapist tells me life is full of unnecessary shoulds."

Mrs. Coover drew her hands away. "Can I see the bedrooms? It's been a long time since I was upstairs here."

"Come on," said Fay. Ruthlessly she flung open the door to her parents' room. It looked tumbled, bluish, and vulnerable, and she felt as if she'd caught someone clutching at a towel in the bathroom.

Next she marched Mrs. Coover to her own room. "Mine's the same as it's always been," she said. She stretched her arm across the door, holding the knob, as Mrs. Coover stepped inside. The room was neat and orderly. Fay was the only member of the family who made her bed in the morning. The pictures she'd had since childhood still hung on the walls. She was safe; the room revealed little about her.

"Here's Natalie's room," and Fay swept open another door, which made a swishing sound over the wall-to-wall carpet. Natalie had insisted on getting the carpet when she was fifteen, saying the random-width oak floors were plain and boring. Now the room exuded a staleness, an intimate married flavor. Detachedly Fay observed Natalie's and Evan's shoes mixed together on the floor, Natalie's blow-dryer and Evan's electric razor tossed on the dresser, a nature magazine folded inside-out on the nightstand.

"What's this?" Mrs. Coover bent down to touch the keyboard of a computer.

"Natalie's gift to Evan. She got it on sale at her company."

"So this is the printer, and this is the thinking part. The main terminal, they call it? I see," said Mrs. Coover disapprovingly. "Was he happy to get it?"

"I guess so. Although he did say, from the size of the box, he was sort of hoping it was exercise equipment."

"Well, we can't always get what we want, can we?" Mrs. Coover seemed pleased.

They came to the door of the guest room, but Fay didn't open the door. "J.J. has this room," she said. "And now you've had the tour."

"Where does *he* sleep?"

"Hoon? He has a cot in Daddy's little office downstairs. We fold it up during the day."

They rejoined the others in the living room. Natalie had hung the flag in front of the fire to dry, on a quilt rack. Fay's mother was tidying up, arranging the Christmas presents into piles. The presents from Hoon and J.J. fascinated Fay. They had given her parents a set of jade carvings, and there were elaborate paper cut-outs for her and Natalie. Fay cradled a jade monkey in her hand, running a finger down its cheek. She wondered what it would be like to be J.J., to be married with a baby, and to leave your husband and child behind to visit a country so far from home. She wondered, not for the first time, if Hoon and J.J. were lovers, and decided they were not. Was that what Mrs. Coover had been trying to find out, upstairs?

She gulped down the last of her cranberry juice, watery now with melted ice. The piles of gifts her mother was making frightened her. How could so many big boxes, wrapped in fancy paper, yield only these trifles? Her father had given her a bottle of sparkling cider and a check that lay nestled in the pocket of the new jumper her mother had sewn. She had given her mother a calendar and a pocketbook. She gave her father a gray wool vest and a bowtie which she now doubted he would wear. She gave Natalie a jewelry box. Natalie wore little jewelry, but the box was pretty and could be used for other things. Fay had found a framed picture of cardinals for Evan, knowing he liked wildlife. Natalie had given each member of the family a stoneware mug, wrapped in paper stamped with praying hands. She had found the mugs and the paper at a religious gift shop, she said.

Fay was relieved that she had remembered to bring presents for Hoon and J.J. Not knowing what they would like, she had selected a leather-bound travel diary for each.

Hoon helped Fay's mother gather the discarded wrapping paper. Natalie tapped the paper in Hoon's hand. "Could you fold that, please? We save it.''

Fay balled up a sheet of the praying hands paper and tossed it into the fire. J.J. moved close to the damp flag and touched it. The center looked drier than the edges.

"Would you like to use our phone? To call your husband?'' Fay asked J.J.

"Thank you, but no, that would be too expensive.''

"No, it wouldn't,'' said Fay.

Fay's father had presented Hoon and J.J. each with a small fossil, a lump of graphite imprinted with prehistoric ferns. They were clearly delighted with the gifts, examining them again and again. Now Fay's father said, "By all means, call your husband!'' but Fay knew he was thinking about the phone bill.

"But it's not Christmas in Taiwan,'' said J.J. "Our holidays are different. To my husband, it's just Tuesday.''

"I wish you could put in a guest appearance in my classroom,'' said Fay. "My students would ask, What holidays do you have?''

"One that we don't have,'' said Hoon, "is Valentine's Day. Instead, we have Broken Hearts Day.''

"That makes a lot more sense,'' said Evan, and everyone looked at him.

Hoon laughed, his eyes crinkling like a jack-o'-lantern's. Fay noticed the gray in his hair. Suddenly she remembered a small paper bag in her coat pocket, and she fetched it from the closet.

"I've got a trick up my sleeve,'' she announced.

"I'll bet you do,'' said Mrs. Coover.

Fay met her gaze. "We need boiling water.'' She held up several colored capsules. Her father took one and inspected it. Fay said, "My students showed me these.''

Evan said, "Drugs! All prep school kids do drugs.''

"It's not drugs,'' said Fay. Mrs. Coover brought a kettle of hot water and poured it into a glass bowl.

"The kids are fascinated with these,'' Fay said.

"Uh-oh,'' said her mother, and they laughed.

Fay selected a purple capsule and tossed it into the bowl of hot water. Everyone crowded around to see.

"What's it doing?'' asked Evan.

The capsule bobbed, then burst, a small sponge working its way outward, blooming into an inch-long purple railroad car. Hoon and J.J. exclaimed; Fay's parents applauded. Fay curtsied. "Show and tell," she said. Mrs. Coover picked up a green capsule and threw it into the bowl. A prim little Christmas tree appeared, its branches triangular.

J.J. lifted the bag and read the label, "Made in Taiwan." Everyone laughed.

"The nation of party favors," said Fay's father, patting Hoon's shoulder.

"It's getting late," said Mrs. Coover. "I guess Christmas is over." Fay's father helped her with her coat. Fay didn't join in the chorus of good-byes as Mrs. Coover vanished through the front door to her own house across the field.

That evening, long after the rest of the family had gone to bed, Fay stayed busy downstairs. She kept heating up water and plopping the capsules into the bowl and removing the sponges to dry on the mantelpiece. In the stillness of the sleeping house, she could hear the pine cones snapping open on the tree, the radiators hissing upstairs and down, the ashes sifting through the grate in the fireplace.

The Christmas stockings, emptied of their treats, hung limply from the mantel. The names "Mom," "Dad," "Natalie," and "Fay" were spelled out in faded sequins on ancient red flannel. Fay remembered her mother making them long ago, when she was about five and Natalie seven.

Long ago . . . and now she was grown. Last Christmas, when Natalie became engaged to Evan, she gave Fay a small carved wooden statue. When Fay asked, "What is it?" Natalie had replied, "The god of hope!" Fay had forced herself to join in the laughter, but even now she had not forgiven Natalie for that.

She placed the sponge Christmas trees together to make a forest and linked the railroad cars into a train. She thought about Sonny Coover, getting married to some unknown girl; soon he'd be a father. She could picture his lean frame and tight-curled blond hair, but not his face. It had been so long since she'd seen him.

Needing more space on the mantelpiece for the trees and the railroad cars, she pushed aside a stack of greeting cards. Beneath them lay last year's Christmas photographs, which she'd scrutinized earlier. With surprise, she realized her father had taken no pictures that day. He must have forgotten.

The water in the bowl was cold, but now she was finished. She picked up the bowl to carry it to the kitchen and was startled to see Hoon watching her from the doorway of the living room. He was wearing a burgundy velour bathrobe and black slippers. She realized she was too tired to smile. She wondered if she and her family had exhausted Hoon and J.J. with their constant smiling and jovial talk, trying to put the visitors at ease.

"Hi," he said.

"Hi. Look at this. Most American families have electric trains, but we've just got these goofy sponges." The interlocking cars fit together to make a long train, which, for his benefit, she now drew through the thicket of small trees on the mantel.

"You are the engine, Fay," he said. "Making it go."

"Am I?" she asked. "Yes, I guess I am." Straight-faced, she looked at him, and he gazed steadily back at her.

The Things That Scare Us

The therapy group met once a week at an old brick church. The group leader, Bill Hatcher, liked to read the tombstones in the little graveyard. His favorite one said, "Gone to be an Angel." On nice days the group sat right there in the graveyard, beneath a huge sycamore tree that dated back to the Civil War, when the church had served as a hospital for troops injured in battles around Memphis, which was fifteen miles away. Bill had seen photographs of the tree in its early years, surrounded by convalescent Confederates. Even then the tree was large, and the soldiers reclining beside it looked somber and lean. Memphis had grown now, but Memphis seemed far away. This was still just an old church in the country, surrounded by stubbly fields and tangled woods.

Bill Hatcher was six-foot-four, swaybacked and thin, his hair just beginning to gray. He knew his overbite kept him from being handsome. Once, he had been sure he would be a basketball player. He had never intended to become a counselor, but it was the only job where people seemed to like him. He had been fired from his previous positions in publishing houses. He hadn't done anything wrong, but always his boss would find some reason to let him go.

Now he worked at a county mental health clinic, and every Tuesday afternoon at five o'clock he came here. The church group had been meeting for several months. Because it was the church his parents belonged to, he felt he couldn't refuse, even though no money was offered. Bill had six participants: the preacher himself—Doug—a young man just out of the seminary; a heavy-set brunette seamstress named DeeDee; a quiet, catlike, one-eyed meter-reader named Ralph; and an older couple, Mr. and Mrs. Cousins, who had a consignment store, selling secondhand clothing and furniture. And there was Laura Guard, whom Bill loved. She ran a doll shop.

The previous week a cicada had come and perched on top of the "Gone to be an Angel" tombstone and had proceeded slowly, slowly, to step out of its old skin, dry its new wings, and fly away. There was excited discussion about how appropriate that was, for the cicada to come and do that while everyone here was pondering how to make changes, how to be happy.

Now a leaf, tinged with yellow, fell into Bill's lap as he sat beneath the tree on a hassock and welcomed everyone. Laura Guard came and sat beside him. She wore a billowing khaki dress, and despite the heat there was a pumpkin-colored scarf wound around her neck and fastened with a pink rhinestone honeybee pin. Her fingers played with the fringe of the scarf. Bill loved her because she was so gentle. She had been hurt in so many ways that the anger was flushed out of her and only the gentleness remained. Her husband had left her; her young son had died in a car crash. She spoke little in the group. Bill suspected that she was still in love with her husband, even though, as far as he knew, they had divorced and she never heard from him anymore. Bill had tried, shyly and without success, to get her to sign up for regular private therapy.

Now she picked up the leaf and smiled, "Always in August, you tell yourself it's just the heat making them yellow. But fall's on the way."

"There's those that won't complain," mumbled Ralph. As usual, he smelled of gasoline.

"Pardon?" said Laura, and Ralph fairly screamed his same reply.

Everyone was there, forming a circle: Bill, DeeDee, Mrs. Cousins, Mr. Cousins, Doug, Ralph, and Laura. It was the Cousinses' turn to bring refreshments, and Mrs. Cousins passed around paper cups and a cooler brimming with sweet chartreuse liquid in which a fly floated. Ralph sipped his, then spat it out and poured the rest of his cupful on the ground. Bill wanted to do likewise, but of course he couldn't. Mrs. Cousins glared balefully at Ralph.

"Who'd like to go first today?" asked Bill, sensing tension, consciously making his voice mild. A long silence was broken only by the sounds of a man mowing the field next to them. Bill looked out at that field, deep with golden shadows; then his gaze wandered to the church marquee, which sat just outside the front door and bore the name of the preacher and the time of the Sunday service. Every week the preacher arranged the plastic letters to spell out a proverb, a saying, or a threat. This week the marquee said, "You think it's hot up HERE?"

As the silence streatched out, Laura Guard ran a hand up under her hair, stroking her scalp. It was her habit. By the end of the hour she would have drawn her hand through her hair many times. Whether her hair was blondish or a sort of tarnished silver, Bill couldn't decide. She must be over forty, he knew, a decade beyond him, yet when he looked at her, years fell away and she was a twenty-year-old girl by a swimming pool. She was slender, though she hid her figure in billows and pleats; her hands were smooth as soap and her cheekbones, though sharp, were not bitter. But ten years older . . . he imagined what his mother would say: "Why, she was already halfway grown when you were still swinging on the moon."

"I'd like to start," the preacher burst out, and everyone looked at him. He seemed ready to cry. He had a high, braying voice, made more strident when he was upset. "I didn't pass my Presbytery exam again, and now I'll have to face the elders and see if they want to keep me on or let me go."

"Of course they'll keep you, Doug," said DeeDee, leaning forward in her lawn chair. Her eyebrows formed an inverted V of concern. Her silo-shaped breasts pressed against her plaid blouse. The blouse had little metallic threads in it, Bill saw.

"No, they won't!" barked the preacher. A horsefly clung to his thin arm, and he swatted at it in fury. "That exam was damned hard, and now I've failed it twice. It's not, 'What was up in the sky on Christmas?' and 'Who was Mary?' It's real difficult stuff.''

"Well," began Mrs. Cousins, "since it's public knowledge that you earn $26,000 a year and only work one day a week, I'd've thought the least you could do was pass some test."

In the shocked silence Bill reflected that, though he bore the preacher no ill will, he couldn't help but agree with Mrs. Cousins. He was amazed that the national council had set such a high salary. And he could tell that Doug just read his sermons out of books.

"It's not your job to criticize him!" cried DeeDee to Mrs. Cousins.

"Somebody has to," Mrs. Cousins replied briskly, pouring herself more of the green drink. Her round, dangling earrings reminded Bill of eyeballs. "First we heard about how scared he was to have taken this job. Then we heard about how nervous he was before the test. Now he's failed it—again. He has to realize that he can pass that test if he puts his mind to it, and then maybe he'll start deserving all that money. As it is now, he's not allowed to do weddings and funerals, so we have to pay somebody else extra to do that."

"Leave me alone!" said the preacher, his face and neck scarlet. "I know my Bible from A to Izzard. I earn that salary!"

Ralph chuckled. "I've got one for you, Doug. How many wise men were there?"

To stem the tide of torment, Bill hastily interposed. "Would everyone take a pencil and paper, and we're going to do something new." His hand touched Laura's cool fingers as he handed her a pencil.

"Self-portrait," said DeeDee, holding her paper up for the group to see. She had drawn a big circle. DeeDee had always been heavy, and now she was pregnant. Her problem, she had told the group weeks earlier, was that she didn't want the baby. She had wanted it at first, when she'd thought the baby's father was going to marry her. But he had left town, and now she was six months along.

"Aww," said Mrs. Cousins. She snatched the paper and drew exaggerated eyes on it, with long lashes. "Your lovely eyes." DeeDee smiled shakily. Forgiveness was in the air, for what Mrs. Cousins had said about Doug. At least DeeDee had forgiven her, but Doug, who sat with his head averted, had not.

"Actually, we're not doing self-portraits today," said Bill, disturbed by the sarcasm in his voice. "I thought we could make lists of the things that frighten us, and talk about that." Bill repeated his role to himself: find out what a person truly wants, and then help him identify specific steps toward achieving it. The list of fears was something the head counselor at the clinic had suggested to Bill and the other staff members. Bill had tried it before with individual patients, finding that the more they talked, the less he had to do. But an inner voice said, It's just a trick, like getting them to make paper swans.

"Things—that—scare—us," said Mr. Cousins slowly, writing the words at the top of his paper. "Not us. Me!" No one laughed. It was typical of what he would say. He was so much in his wife's shadow that people paid him little attention.

Mrs. Cousins joked, "We used to be afraid our crabapples would get all eaten up by mealybugs. But I put some cut white potatoes nearby, and now the bugs go to the taters instead."

Pencils scratched on paper. Ralph took off one shoe, held it on his lap, and used the sole as a surface to write against. Mrs. Cousins ticked her tongue. The preacher sat with his arms folded, not writing. Laura Guard bent over her list; Bill couldn't see her face. She was so quiet. He never forgot she was there, though the others just talked around her.

While they wrote, Bill pondered his own fears, terrors that multiplied like mealybugs. He was afraid of so many things: of never getting married. Of always being poor. Of losing his parents. He dreaded feeling lonely or frantic or just blue, because he felt that way so often, and each time it happened it was terrible. He was afraid of failure, especially with women. He ruined all of his opportunities with them. He remembered a cute girl who used to live in his apartment building. She'd invited him in for brownies; before he knew it, he'd eaten the whole plate of them, not leaving a single one for her, while he talked about his job search. She'd looked disgusted. Her face clearly said, "Hog!" That was how it always was with women—his titanic insecurity. He couldn't be himself around them.

Except with Laura, in his dreams. He felt protective toward her. She was the kind of person that a wild rabbit would let come up and pet it.

"Things that scare you," Bill began, breaking the silence. "Frighten you, shock you, unnerve you. Talking about them will help. Let's start with DeeDee, at my left, and go around the circle."

DeeDee crossed her legs at the knee and swung her foot nervously. "So many things scare me, I don't hardly know where to begin. Mainly this kid. I'm afraid that after it's born, I won't be happy anymore. I'm afraid it won't have a good life growing up. I'm afraid I'll never see Rodney, the baby's father, again, and that I won't ever have any more boyfriends."

Mr. Cousins said, "Young, pretty girl like you! Lots of men would be proud to marry you." Mrs. Cousins goggled at her husband.

DeeDee burst into tears. "So why didn't Rodney? He said he loved me. Said it the day the mall gave away free ice cream. There was a child's plastic swimming pool set up in front of Woolworth's, all filled with ice cream sundaes, and while we were eating ours, Rodney said he loved me. And then he left. But that's not all I feel bad about. My doctor says it might be twins."

Mr. Cousins said, "Then I have just the thing for you—a double-wide stroller our daughter-in-law wants to get rid of." He held his hands wide apart. "When you walk down the street, everybody'll move aside for you. They'll have to!"

Magically, DeeDee's tears dried. She looked at Mr. Cousins with hope.

Mrs. Cousins cleared her throat. "I'm next. Now, hubby here always says I'm shy," she patted Mr. Cousins' leg, "and the truth is, I have more fears than anybody else I know. Some days I get nervous just wondering what to fix for supper! Why should that be? Whatever I fix is OK with hubby." Mr. Cousins nodded emphatically. "But I worry about these pains in my joints and a feeling in my chest like somebody put a firecracker in it. I'm diabetic," she declared, "and I'm scared of getting AIDS. The needles I use are the throwaway kind, but what if a person with AIDS works at the needle factory and uses one, just to be mean? But mostly I worry about bad gossip. I've always been real careful about my reputation, scared somebody would stab me the back, so to speak. But y'all wouldn't do that," and she swept the circle slowly with her small eyes. "We're all good Christians." She fixed Ralph with a concentrated frown.

Bill said, "Everything we say here is confidential, Mrs. Cousins, but now is a good time to reassure ourselves that nothing we say here goes beyond this group."

"Not beyond the shade of this sycamore tree," murmured Laura. Mrs. Cousins regarded Laura, then the tree, with suspicion, as if the branches concealed a scribbling reporter.

"If anybody says anything bad about my wife, they'll have to answer to me," said Mr. Cousins primly. (Bill thought Laura smiled at this, but he wasn't sure.) "My number one fear is losing her. Everyday I pray the Lord will see fit to make the diabetes go away."

Mrs. Cousins bridled at this, beaming. Then her face changed. "And we're afraid the store mascot, our parrot, Tut-Tut, might die," she added, as if amending a prayer. "He keeps pecking at his feet."

Bill checked his watch, wondering why he ever worried about filling up the hour. Certain group members were always so very talkative that he often had to cut them short.

"My wife and Tut-Tut, they're my life," said Mr. Cousins. He pulled at his beard, as short and evenly trimmed as carpet fiber. "And our son and his wife and their two little boys, though they don't visit us as much as they ought to, and that breaks my heart and my wife's too. But this is a list of things that scare you, and heartbreak's on another list."

It was Doug's turn. "Nuclear war. Although that could have a good side effect—people might start praying again." His small jaw was set as if to say, Bring on the bombs.

"Oh Doug, nobody thinks about nuclear war!" protested DeeDee.

Bill said nothing, realizing not only that he hated to talk about nuclear war, but that he disliked anyone who did. While the preacher lectured the group about radioactivity and its attendant dangers, Bill thought about Laura's doll shop. It was only a few blocks from his clinic, and he sometimes glimpsed her through the window, arranging the wide-eyed dolls on the shelves. They were old fashioned, with snowy pinafores, jointed arms, and coils of glossy hair, and their serious porcelain faces suggested lives of compelling truth. Once he'd bought a doll there for his seven-year-old niece. It was a boy doll in a complete suit of football clothes, including tiny plastic shoulder pads, a red jersey, matching red breeches, and soft black plastic shoes that pulled on over the doll's stiff feet. "And little red socks," Laura had said happily. But Bill's niece disliked the doll, saying she preferred "regular pretty ones."

Bill realized that Doug was finished talking about war. A restless silence prevailed, and Bill thought he felt a raindrop on his forehead. He prompted, "Ralph?"

"My worry is more crucial than unwanted babies and nuclear war. It's the general trend toward rudeness in this country. I read an article about it."

"But *you* are rude, Ralph," challenged Mrs. Cousins. "Pouring my limeade on the ground!"

"Interruptions, for example." Ralph nodded at her, his good eye narrowed, his scent of gasoline strong. "One person breaking into the speech of another. That's the form of rudeness that people in a survey said they hated most of all."

"I wasn't interrupting!" said Mrs. Cousins. "It's just give and take in these sessions."

"Give and take, that's right," said DeeDee. "I think you're afraid to open up, Ralph."

While Ralph took out a handkerchief and blew his nose, Bill said, "Nobody has to open up more than they want to."

"Exactly," Ralph said. "Everybody's got problems. It's rude and selfish to complain all the time, and that in my opinion is what everybody here needs to learn. But since all of you-all are waving your dirty underwear in public, I'll give you something to think on. I'm afraid my garbage collector might stop coming. We had an argument about the way he leaves stuff all over the place—pieces of paper and tin cans and God knows what else that falls off his truck. Yet he wants everything wrapped up tidy in plastic bags. I said, To hell with gift-wrapped garbage. So I taught him a lesson. When I heard his truck coming, I hid myself in my biggest can, with the lid over me. When he lifted off that lid, I jumped out and yelled at him and spit. Well, he hasn't come back, and now I've got so much garbage I'll have to take it to the dump myself.'' Dejectedly he motioned toward his pickup truck. ''Loaded up before I came.''

DeeDee clamored, ''Serves you right!'' Doug piped up, ''If that's your big worry, would you like some of mine?'' Mrs. Cousins rumbled, ''*I've* never had any trouble with *my* garbageman.''

Mr. Cousins added, ''He's like a member of the family.''

Laura was laughing, softly at first, then harder, her hands over her mouth, rocking back and forth. It was the first time Bill had seen her laugh like this, and he was enthralled. He, too, laughed, out of pure joy. Then Mr. Cousins was saying, ''Hey, it's raining,'' and the preacher said, ''Our time's up.'' In truth it was raining, drops spattering down through the jade leaves of the sycamore tree, and there was the strong headwind of a thunderstorm, blowing their skirts and pantlegs hard against their knees.

''What are you scared of, Laura?'' demanded DeeDee, folding her plastic chair flat.

''Being struck by lightning,'' Laura cried.

Mrs. Cousins' hair, layered in an artichoke style, stood up in the wind. She touched Laura's shoulder. ''You be careful, girl. I had a bad dream about you. I dreamed you died.''

The group scattered, each person with a lawn chair, Ralph loping to his laden truck, the Cousinses hurrying to their shiny new car, DeeDee setting off, flatfooted, to her house down the road, Doug scurrying back into the church. In seconds Bill and Laura stood alone under the tree. Her face was blank and vulnerable, shellshocked, like the expressions of the sick Confederates in old photographs.

Love and pity welled up in Bill's heart. He said, "Don't pay one bit of mind to that ignorant old biddy."

"I'm glad I didn't get my turn." Her voice was rapid and light. She jerked at the ends of her pumpkin-colored scarf. "I don't like to talk about fears. When my husband said, Let's stay married but see other people, I wondered, How can I go on? All kinds of innocent things became edged in awfulness, like a tuna sandwich on the kitchen counter or the feeling of blankets at night. Everything turned into fear. And then a year later he left me. Even now I wonder, What did I do to make him go away? Have you ever seen dry ice, Bill? At picnics, people pack cold drinks in it."

He nodded, held by her amber-flecked eyes, his professionalism shattered by emotion.

"It changes from a solid into a gas, never going through the liquid stage in between. I wanted to be able to change like that, to skip the middle stage, which is pain."

"You deserve all of the good, Laura, and none of the bad."

"But I'm afraid the phone will ring. I'm afraid I won't remember which way to turn out of this driveway to go home. I'm a quiet person, and I like quiet things. I still hurt. Once, I was away from my house for a long time and when I got back, it was winter. I found twenty dead birds in my woodstove. They had flown down the flue to get warm, and they died. It was my fault, because I hadn't thought to put a screen over the chimney! But you, Bill . . . are you afraid of anything?"

The wind shirred through the big tree. A blackbird sang a short, distressed tune; thunder sounded. He would say it. He would. He gathered his breath. "Of never getting to tell you how much I admire you."

With two fingers she brushed his cheek, and he stood so still that his muscles were rock, or air. "It's all right," she said.

She turned away, batting raindrops from her face, and sprinted across the grass. Bill watched while she tucked her small body into her old car, backed out of the parking lot, and drove down the hill and away, looking like one of her dolls behind the wheel. Her taillights flashed in the rain.

The blackish fringe of the sycamore leaves flapped against the sky. Bill gathered up the pencils and scraps of paper that lay on the ground, the discarded lists of fears. He recognized Ralph's handwriting, and that of Mr. Cousins. Ralph had put, "pick-pockets." Mr. Cousins had scrawled: "that there will be a wasp on the toilet seat because I was stung there once." Other lists said: losing my family, dying, getting sick or crippled, growing old, not having enough money.

He felt that he had failed to help anyone today. He told himself, I should stop having these meetings. Next week, I'll tell them it's the last time. Next week, or the week after that.

He had, in fact, no idea how to help the preacher overcome his fear of nuclear war or Mrs. Cousins her dread of catching AIDS. Or were those fears a kind of security for them, something to hang onto, to blame?

He asked himself, What do I want? and he imagined everyone in the group—Mr. and Mrs. Cousins, DeeDee, Ralph, the preacher, Laura—all smiling, their mouths wide open, growing and changing, their homely human terrors resolved at last.

Passionately he wanted Laura to come rolling back up the drive-way in her rusty car and invite him to supper. They could go any-where, a fast-food chicken place, and she would be dreamy and kind, laughing the way she had laughed a short time before.

He waited, but she didn't come. After a while, as the rain fell harder, he drove away.

Malta Fever

We're sinking, I can tell. We're a string quartet, our folding chairs perched atop a tuffet of marshy earth, surrounded by a man-made moat. We share the tuffet with a huge elm tree whose broken top and brown-tipped leaves declare, "Root-rot." And no wonder, living as it does in this weird little pond. Anybody can tell the tree was here before the moat was, and the tree is mortally offended. But the rest of the quartet—Cynthia, Clarence, and Joe—don't seem to be thinking about anything but our quavery rendition of "Christmas Is Coming, the Goose is Getting Fat." (Christmas is *not* coming; it's only August.) If the marshy oval where we're sitting begins to split apart, or drops any lower into the moat, I'll stick my viola into its case, hold it over my head, and scream until help arrives. I can't swim. Never mind the fact that the moat is only five yards across—it's deep and it smells bad. You could get swamp fever just by looking at it.

We're playing eighteenth-century music for an eighteenth-century picnic, a fundraiser for the Fair Haven Historical Society. We won't be paid for this, damn it, but we'll at least receive a free supper. Our audience, watching us from just across the moat, is consuming these suppers out of little baskets. I understand they paid dearly for those baskets, and I want mine, I'm hungry.

It's a sticky, humid evening, with sky the color of ice. No sign of Kannon Andrews (my lover) among the picnickers; he must be playing croquet up at the mansion. His mother's family used to own the mansion, but now it's funded by the society and all sorts of grants, and Kannon's mother, Lana, acts as its live-in caretaker. She's got it made, living in the house rent free and getting paid just for being there. And what a place it is. God. A house with ten bedrooms, acres and acres of fruit trees—apple, pear, cherry, fig (Lana makes halfway decent fig preserves)—and a field that grows the best watermelons in the world, the small round emerald-green kind that you can't find in stores anymore.

Our music ends. Music? Who am I kidding? I've heard better sounds from windshield wipers. Was it just me? Joe and Clarence, seasoned violinists and buddies of mine, throw me looks of sympathy, pack up, and scurry off. Cynthia, the flutist, swivels toward me. Her curls, long and narrow and tight like telephone cords, bounce over her shoulders. Her broad nose keeps jumping as she rebukes me: "See what happens when you miss rehearsal, Allison?"

"Oh, eat your flute." I've got to get to dry land. Thank God, there's Kannon hurrying toward me across the rickety bridge, smiling, though because he's wearing sunglasses the shape, size, and opacity of bottlecaps, I can't see his eyes, even when we kiss.

Where did that breeze come from? A playful zephyr snatches a sheet of music off a stand—Cynthia's music—and flings it out onto the moat, where it floats apathetically beside a clump of what looks like the eggs of a miniature monster. Cynthia's "Noooo!" has six or seven syllables.

"Cheated of their human snack," I say, "the octopi of the deep seek revenge on the one who has irked them most."

"Oh, for God's sake, Allison." Cynthia hates me, she really does. And I hate her more than anyone else in the world except Kannon's mother.

"Where's a stick?" asks Kannon. He snaps a branch off the elm tree and reaches out with it, but the paper eludes him. Why is he helping Cynthia? He knows how I feel about her. But before I know it, he's skinning off his shoes, rolling up his trouser legs, and wading into the mire, which promptly swallows him up to the waist. He retrieves the soggy paper, waves it over his head, and slides back onto the central tuffet, where Cynthia is waiting, if not with arms outstretched, at least with a smug smile.

"Thank you, Kannon. My grandmother gave me that piece. I would have hated most terribly to lose it."

"You're welcome, Cynthia, I—"

"Leech check," I say, circling him. Slick black weeds nestle in the waistband of his once-white slacks, but why am I bothering with him? He just betrayed me, and his bikini-style underwear, showing through the wet trousers, reveals him for the fool he is. I head for shore, my feet carumphing over the makeshift bridge.

When I look back, Kannon is straddling the folding chair I left behind, and Cynthia's picking leaves off him with all the enthusiasm of someone changing a bedpan, but for her, that's loving kindness.

Loyalty is all I ask, but Kannon's heart is so hard it dents any probe. Just recently I tested his devotion this way: Would he agree to spit on the ground on a certain date, annually and forever?

"Why?"

"Because, Kannon, it's the birthday of someone I hate."

"You're talkin' rituals, you're talkin' long-term . . ." he shuffled his feet, summoning the three-eighths of redneck in his blood.

"I'd do it for you! I do lots of things for people I love."

"Yeah? I've never seen you spit. And if this is Cynthia you're talking about, why not get out of the damn quartet?"

"Because I was in it before she ever came on the scene! Joe took her on in a weak moment."

"Allison? Have you eaten yet?" Lana, Kannon's mother, cuts through my reverie and hands me a basket. "That's free, but you'll have to pay a quarter for something to drink."

I hand over a quarter for a cup of lemonade. Kannon joins me and we sit on the ground, near the croquet field, and uncover the basket to discover a soggy croissant, a wedge of ammoniac Brie, very wet pressed turkey, and what appears to be white mustard. I spread the mustard on the turkey, put it in the croissant, and take a big bite. It's not mustard: it's cheesecake, melted.

Here's some background. When Kannon and I first started seeing each other, a year ago, it was grand; he begged for my attention, and I was loyal as I knew how, and reassuring. I told him, "If I ever leave you, you'll know why."

These days, though, he slips away from intimacy like an eel. Picking through my disappointing supper, I examine his profile; fish eyed, he avoids my stare.

Lana bends over us, her basset hound face level with mine, her shorts riding up her thighs. She's too old to be wearing anything that shows her knees. "Well, your quartet did a right creditable job," she says.

"Thanks, Lana."

"Kannon," she asks, "who's that pretty girl you were helping over there?" Lana has a burbly southern accent, heavily iambic.

"Cynthia. She's in the quartet too, Ma."

"I can see that. It was real nice of you to help her, son."

"Lana, you just take the cake," I say. "Want a joint? I've got some real fine pot in my pocketbook. It would do you good, hon."

She stumps off so fast I expect her to spin right into the ground, like a drill.

"You're not helping things, Allison."

"There are too many people around, Kannon, and this dinner sucks. Would you go get me another croissant out of one of those unclaimed baskets? That's the only edible thing in here."

"You get mad when I do anything with anybody else."

"I wasn't mad when you were just playing croquet."

"If we ever got married, I'd end up sleeping on the sofa half the time, either bummed out or kicked out."

He said it. He said the word; there's hope. I wipe the cheese-cake off my fingers and squeeze his hand. "Sofas can be comfortable, Kannon. Never rule out anything on account of a sofa."

The bad thing (one of the bad things) is that we work together. We teach psychology, and some time ago, when the flames of love burned more brightly, we embarked on a joint project: a study of bullies. We hand-picked them from the playground and asked their parents if the children could participate in a study of "passive/aggressive behavior." Can't the parents see they've raised a bully?

But no, they're proud: "Yes, my son has a real strong sense of himself." We've got permission slips on ten or twelve of them, which is more than enough meanness to do a study on. But our department chairman wants to know why the bully study is taking so long to finish. You've had all summer, he says. That's the best time, with the kids out of school. Where ya been? Whatcha been doin'? The rate you're going you'll be studying bad grownups. No thanks, I tell him, I see too many of those as it is.

It's the day after the picnic, the last Saturday in August. I overslept, so I reach the office late, and Kannon and the bullies are already there. He's sweating, the bullies are chewing their lips and lazily swatting each other, and the last parent is departing. The office that Kannon and I share is big and sunny, with desks on each side of the room and a furry orange rug. The bullies, five boys, four girls, are jumbled together on the rug, except for two who fight for the swivel chair at my desk. Kannon's face looks fat and tired this morning. Why do I fool with him? That outmoded beard, a queer-looking shirt Lana gave him for Flag Day, and using my coffee mug again because it's clean.

"Want to start?" he asks me.

"Hi, I'm Allison Brown." The bullies pick their noses, beetle their brows at me. "And this is Kannon Andrews. We're just going to do some talking this morning, and then we have cookies and Kool-Aid for you. Hey," I say to the two fighting over the swivel chair, "chill out or I'll make you sit on your heads."

Kannon says, "We, uh, would like to know how you decide who to play with."

"Kannon, that's not the question we should start with. Remember what we're dealing with here." I scan the group; a red-haired monster squints up at me. I ask her, "For instance, do you pinch people?"

"You mean like this? Yeah, I pinch till it turns white." Red-hair pinches a big-big girl next to her, who retaliates with a slap. Suddenly the orange rug is a combat zone, an epidemic of pinches and slaps.

"Allison! Allison! Let's stick to our plan!" Kannon passes me a clipboard with questions written on it: What is a friend? What kinds of people do you like? What kinds do you dislike? "Kids, just play. Just talk with each other. Here," he fishes change from his pocket and tosses it on the floor.

Instantly, the floor is a battleground of fists and teeth and yelling. Feet grind into hands, fingers twist locks of hair, T-shirts are pulled till they stretch. "That's *mine! I've* got that quarter!"

Kannon is taking notes furiously, now and then stopping to pick up his camera and snap a picture. I say, "Kannon, we're going to have to do this individually. What we have here is a group dynamics thing."

"I can't hear you," he says behind his camera.

"Knock knock," comes a voice at the door. "Goodness, what a playful group!" It's Cynthia, leaning into the room, her fleshy nose topped with pointy sunglasses, a big saggy pocketbook dangling from her shoulder, a flute in her hand. Her stinky green-smelling perfume fills the office.

"Cynthia!" Kannon bounds over to greet her.

"Is our lunch date still on?" she asks.

"Um. Sure. Do you want to meet me there, or should I pick you up?"

I can't believe this. I won't. Instinct says: Fight back! "Kids," I announce, "that lady in the doorway keeps Milky Way bars in her purse. Lots of them! She came here specially to give them to you." Warily the bullies rise from the rug, then surge toward Cynthia, their hands out, amid a rising din.

"It's not true!" she cries. "I don't have any candy!"

"She likes to play tag, kids! She'll give a Milky Way to anybody who can chase her down the hall and touch her on the back of the neck!"

Cynthia screams, and they're off. Kannon holds back one or two, but they struggle away, breaking free. He goes bounding after them, and in seconds I'm all alone.

I crash their wedding. As Lana and I spread fig preserves on thin little biscuits at the buffet table, I say, "It's just that sex with him was so good."

Lana's false fingernails look like pistachio seeds; one of them falls off. "You did everything wrong. You'll have to give up now."

Weaving through the guests, I step outside. It's cold, looks like it's about to snow. A hundred yards away, beside the now frozen pond, Kannon and Cynthia are cavorting on the winter grass. Her wedding dress is a weird shape, tight around her hips and flared out at the feet. They don't see me.

I know what I should have done: I should have gotten Malta fever. My grandmother had it as a young girl, an undulating fever that sends you in and out of consciousness; it won my grandfather back when he'd started to roam.

But some things you don't think of in time, or they're just not your style.

I watch Kannon and Cynthia skip across the frozen pond to the tuffet of earth and embrace there. He lifts her up and swings her round and round until they collapse beneath the bare elm tree, her white veil rising around them like a giant mushroom. They kiss.

My champagne glass sparkles in my hand. The fig preserves tastes just like smoke.

Out There

Christy thought about her heart a lot, about how it felt to be herself: her heart was a kernel of popcorn, just about to pop. Her heart was a morsel of meat being grasped by terrible claws. Her heart was a dark wingspan, a terrible shadow cast by the prehistoric bird—archaeopteryx?—that had haunted her childhood nightmares.

She was thirty-two. Tall, sturdily built, black haired. She had a wide clown-smiling mouth and hazel eyes that filled too easily and too often, and she had a newspaper job in Richmond. She made her home with her grandmother a few miles outside the city because there it was quiet. She'd never married, because the men who were beguiled by her trembling mouth and her big, uncertain eyes grew puzzled by her once they knew her, and they went away. At night she lay awake listening to her heart beating their names into her ears. She couldn't laugh at them, and when she thought about how they turned away from her, she pressed her hands to her eyes in the dark, until her own face was as set and mild as the faces of the men who had found they couldn't love her.

There was a man named Deems, who worked with her, whom she feared. At night she imagined his hollow footsteps pegging down the hall toward her room, and she fell asleep with the sense that, at any moment, his hands would be around her neck. One evening after work he took her out to dinner. When she spilled her glass of wine, he smiled and mopped it up for her, and after dinner they went back to his apartment downtown. He lit a candle and found some music on the radio, and they danced very slowly, while the traffic honked in the street outside his dark window and the streetlights changed color on the room's old wallpaper. When Deems asked her why she was afraid, she didn't want to hurt his feelings by telling him that she feared him. She didn't know what he'd do if she told him.

She broke away from him, snatched her coat from the closet where he'd hung it, and raced down the steps. She heard him calling after her. When she crossed the street, she looked back and saw him framed at the window, now brilliantly lighted. She wondered if she should return, murmur Sorry, pick up the dance step again. Her lips twitched, but she didn't go back.

"You shouldn't be living out here with me," her grandmother often told her. "You'd be better off in town, and I'd be perfectly all right by myself."

Christy didn't care whether her grandmother lived there or not. She just liked the silence of the big house, and the trees and grass, and there was even a fishpond thick with last fall's leaves. Her grandmother had hired a man to clean the pond now that it was spring. She said the man had simply walked up the driveway and asked for work.

Christy saw him the morning after he was hired. It was warm for March in Virginia. As she got into her car to go to work, she saw the man taking a rake and a bucket from the toolshed. He didn't seem to see her through the thinly budding trees surrounding the pond. He was as tall as she was, maybe a little younger, with red hair. She touched her own hair. She'd noticed a few quills of white sprouting in its darkness. The man's shoulders hunched over the rake as he lifted out the matted leaves, the dead lotus-flowers long since blackened and bitten by frost, and then he swung a long-handled butterfly net through the cold still water to catch the fish. She watched as he scooped up several of the big spotted goldfish and flicked them into a plastic trashcan that served as a holding tank, and then she slammed her car door and drove past him. He raised his head as she went by.

At work, Deems sat on her desk. "How about another game of

hide-and-seek?'' he asked.

She said she was sorry about their previous evening. But was she really sorry? She didn't like his long thin blond hair or his thick eyelids or his ruddy cheeks that always looked as if they'd just been rubbed with snow. When he leaned forward and tucked a strand of hair behind her ear, something turned inside her. Her mind blocked out the other people moving nearby between the filing cabinets and the glassed-in cubicles, and she caught his hand and held it.

"So!" he said. His fingers squeezed her wrist.

She flinched, dropping his hand and drawing her elbows against her sides. She couldn't bear it if he laughed at her. She thumped her typewriter, rifled a stack of papers. "I'm on deadline." She could never cut out the ground beneath his feet.

When her car wouldn't start that afternoon, it was Deems who took her home. She sat far across the seat from him and said, "You'll get to meet my grandmother. We live in a trailer with geese running around it, and we go barefoot all the time. Howling at the moon."

He looked at her quizzically, not amused, and her face grew hot. As they approached the house, they saw two figures over by the fishpond: her grandmother and the hired man. Her grandmother's henna head bobbed, and she waved her arms. The man stood unmoving beside her.

"My grandmother's eighty years old," Christy told Deems. "She doesn't like me very much."

They joined the others. The hired man said to Christy, "Your grandmother says she lost something in the pond last year, but I'm almost done cleaning, and I haven't found anything."

"What did you lose?" Christy asked her grandmother, but the old woman wouldn't tell. Christy thought how characteristic that was, her grandmother's secrecy, the way she created mystery out of nothing. Maybe she hadn't lost anything at all. Christy didn't remember any such occurrence during the past year. But it had been several years since the pond had been cleaned; maybe the old woman was remembering from a long time ago.

They gazed into the pond, now drained except for a few skims of darkly pooled water strewn with leaves. The light wind chilled them, but they lingered outside becaue the air smelled of freshly bruised grass and thawed earth, and because the hired man was beginning to fill the pond again. Christy wondered suddenly about the way men and women age differently. The hired man, about thirty, might still be called a boy, but she, at thirty-two, would never again be called a girl. He hauled the green hose out from the small toolshed with the peeling white paint, and when he returned to the shed and wrenched the spigot, water spurted into the pond.

"Turn it off!" cried the old woman. "We haven't found what I lost yet." She bent and lifted the hose from the pond. When the man said he'd searched all he could, she turned the nozzle toward him, spraying him. Deems laughed.

"You'd better do as she says," Christy told the hired man, and even as he ran to turn the spigot off, the old woman spun toward Christy and waved the hose up and down over her, soaking her. Christy screamed for her to stop, and the water dwindled to a trickle as the hired man closed off the flow.

"How dare you!" Christy hissed, but this time all three of the others laughed.

"Don't be so sensitive," Deems said.

Christy didn't think it was funny, and she sat through supper with her hair dripping water onto her plate. She wasn't hungry for the cold roast beef served with wild onions, picked by her grandmother, so she pushed her plate away and went outside in her lightweight jacket. She'd already changed her clothes, but she carried a kitchen towel to dry her hair.

The hired man was sitting on cinderblocks beside the pond, eating fried chicken from a cardboard box; there was a fast-food restaurant down the road.

"I think my grandmother's lying about losing something," she said.

"I believe her. I tend to believe what people say."

"Where'd you come from?"

"Been working around here for the past couple years. I'd like to be a full-time gardener.'' He pitched a chicken bone into the bushes.

"That's unusual,'' said Christy. "Who's got the money to pay for that? We sure don't. Besides, this pond work isn't really gardening, it's just labor.''

She decided his face was shaped like a shoebox. He sat clumsily on the cinderblocks, and she told herself that she was only being fair to him.

"I don't care so much about money,'' he said. "Maybe I just like working.''

"Wish I felt that way.'' She wanted to mock him, but something about his face kept the sarcasm out of her voice.

Her glance fell on the large plastic trashcan, the temporary fish container, and she knelt down to examine the gold-scaled creatures swimming along the sides of the can in serene bafflement: spotted mutants, some of them six inches long.

"I call them rogues,'' she said, "because they're not domesticated anymore. They're not what they're supposed to be.''

Gradually she became aware that her back was getting warm. She turned, and the man started up behind her. He had been leaning over her so closely that their bodies almost touched. He, too, had been looking at the fish. She gasped, alarmed at his nearness.

"She lost a locket. She told me, she just didn't tell you,'' the man said. He turned away from her and began to walk down the driveway.

"Where're you going?'' she cried, and then he was sprinting. By the time she got back to the house and summoned her grandmother and Deems, the man was gone.

"I bet he stole my locket,'' the grandmother said. "That's what I lost.''

"Thief!'' Christy cried. She forgot about the dousing her grandmother had given her. Deems took them searching in his car. They strained their eyes along the road for the man, but it was getting dark and they saw no sign of him, so they went back home.

The old woman's hands danced in front of her. "It had a thick gold chain like a braid, and a lovely gold case.''

Christy knew the old woman wanted her to ask whose picture

was inside, but she said nothing. Her grandmother had had so many lovers—at least she claimed she had. She had used them to torment one another, to torment her husband. Christy had heard the stories. Sometimes, her grandmother still went to visit the widow of a man with whom she'd had an affair while her own husband was still alive. The other woman was old too. Christy had accompanied her grandmother on one such visit, wondering why the other woman, as fierce as a sick eagle, tolerated her grandmother, serving her lemon cookies and parrying her barbs. Christy said to herself, I'll never be that way.

"Shouldn't we find out who that guy was?" she asked.

"We don't know for sure that he found that locket," Deems said. "You ladies have assumed the worst about him."

Christy pictured the water bleaching the gold out of the locket, the gold seeping into the scales of the fish. Her grandmother went back inside, but Christy knew she'd be trying to watch her and Deems from a window.

In the darkness Deems placed his hands on either side of Christy's head. She tried to see his face: his mouth looked soft and cruel. "I fixed your car this morning so it wouldn't run," he said, "so I could bring you home."

"I don't like the way things are between us. I don't see what we have in common." Her voice came out hoarsely; she tried to pull away. She told herself, I don't feel anything more for him than I did for that hired man, who I saw for a total of about forty-five minutes and who's now gone forever.

Deems's hands slid to her neck, his strong thumbs pressing beneath her ears. She tilted her head back, letting him kiss her for a long time. He caressed her back, her hips. Her own hands dangled at her sides, and then she rebelled.

"Stop!" she said. "Please stop."

"Goddamn you, Christy." He released her forcibly, so that she fell back, her legs striking something heavy and hard. The trashcan! It toppled over, spilling fish. They flipped and twisted on the grass, and in the dim light Christy could see only mica-like flecks of gold on their scales. Helplessly, she cupped them in her cold hands and sought to move them back to safety. But the trashcan was empty, all the water flooding the small space of grass where she clutched at the fish.

"Deems, help me! They'll die! Get the hose!" Where was he? She stumbled to her feet. "Oh, don't go!" she begged. "You've got to help me now!"

She could see his shape in the darkness. For such a big man, he moved slowly, and she cried, "Hurry, go to the shed and turn on the water!" The many fish flashed darkly in the grass, making a wet, floppy sound. She was crying. She bent down, her shoes sinking into the ground, and waited for water to flow from the hose.

But none came.

"Deems?" She strained her eyes, her ears, searching the dark garden for him. All she saw were black trees, straggling hedges. Her voice broke: "Deems, Deems, don't you hear me?"

Hetty Hawken

In a town with little color, Hetty Hawken was colorful, so she stood out. Her short curls whirled around her ears, her eyes were teal blue, and her nose was long like a collie's. She wore fringed shawls and peasant-style skirts patterned in red and yellow. All this, against a background of gray. She came to the coal-mining town as a schoolteacher. The place she came from was in Tennessee, and so tiny no one had heard of it. But still her hometown was larger than this western Virginia coal town.

The main street, where she had a second-floor apartment in an old building, was lined with bland, crumbling houses. Hetty smelled cabbage and sausage cooking, heard desultory traffic, TV programs drifting through open windows, children's yelps and parents' reprimands.

The town was ringed with coal heaps, and they alone were beautiful, like piles of black diamonds or shattered starlight. Beyond the heaps lay the mountains, long, tired ridges furred with trees, resembling porcupines with thinned quills. Prominent among them was a hill with a notch in its side, like a missing eye.

Hetty taught English at the high school. After the first week she thought, What am I doing here? And how can I get away?

But she had no money, and she was only twenty-two, so she had few choices. Already it was growing cold. The weeds in the sidewalks went to seed. She woke to find frost on the inside of her windows.

On her brisk morning walks to school, who did she see? There was Miss Hopkins, a wraith with dirty hair and terrible sharp breath, who lived in the apartment below Hetty's. There were children who taunted each other, shouting smut as they waited for the bus, and a fat man who owned a gas station. Most notably, a retarded man wandered about reciting the license plates of passing cars: "Dee arr ay nine oh! Pee ell jay seven eight!" His pointless shouting worked on Hetty's nerves. She wondered why no one stopped him.

She taught until three-thirty, straightened her desk and planned lessons until five, and faced the long evenings tired and baffled. Her one luxury was a nightly bubble bath.

She looked for friends among the other teachers, but they were old and brittle, smelling of menthol cough drops, filling the faculty lounge with talk of garden mulch and illness. Or they were middle aged, bossy, nosy, turning her inside out with questions. There was only one other young teacher, Carolyn Foreman. In the restroom one day, Carolyn Foreman crayoned a new lipstick on her mouth, then swore as it snapped in two. Eagerly, Hetty volunteered, "Carolyn, just melt the raw ends a little with a candle, stick them back together, and put it in the freezer for a couple hours."

"Yeah?" said Carolyn. She tossed the lipstick into the trash, clicked her purse shut, and walked away.

Hetty met David Mercer at the one coffee shop in town, noticing him because of the way he was dressed: a black jersey, crisscrossed by suspenders embroidered with laughing and crying theatrical masks. She smiled; his eyes lit up. He was blond, with an open face. He introduced himself and joined her in the torn vinyl booth, his coffee spilling into the saucer. He worked at a store that sold denim jackets and jeans. He was twenty-five, but he hadn't been to college, he said; he'd worked at the store for five years and felt very old.

"Old!" she laughed. "Why do you stay here, then?"

"Don't say that out loud. If people realize they have a choice, my God, by tomorrow this could be a ghost town. The truth is, I'd like to buy a farm around here someday."

"The agrarian impulse."

"The world is folding in on itself. The only way to go forward is to go back to the ways that have worked before. Do you like cows and goats?"

"Is that how you ask for a date? You're the first man to pay any attention to me in this town, and you ask me if I like cows and goats! Is this how people around here pop the question?"

He was laughing, his teeth white and even. "What if I am? Would you say yes?"

"People around here get married right after the senior prom, don't they? So I'm already an old maid. Everybody would think you couldn't do any better!"

"Help me. What do you like? I mean, you deserve something more exotic than an evening at the pinball arcade."

On paper napkins, they exchanged phone numbers.

"I like country music," she said. And she liked him, because he had made her laugh.

They went canoeing, the Clinch River still and wide around them. David steered to the middle, dropped the oars into the boat, and surprised her by producing an apple pie.

"Ever had pie in the middle of a river, Hetty? I'll show you that even here, there's lots you've never done before."

"I can't swim too well. Maybe I shouldn't be out here." Hetty squinted up at the sky, whitish like the last light of a TV set that had been turned off in a dark room. All around them the water spread out in black ripples. She dipped her hand in: it was cold. Theirs was the only boat in sight. Both riverbanks looked far away, the houses along them small and precarious.

The water frightened her, but she was determined not to show it. She bit into the pie. "Mmm, cinnamon. Do you know, this is the first time I haven't felt like I was being watched?"

"You'll always be watched, Hetty. When you pass the window of my shop, customers quit flipping through the jeans and look at you instead."

"But I don't like it! The other teachers, the principal, not my students so much but—oh, those repulsive people I see on my way to work!"

"Like who?"

"That fatso at the gas station, for one. Those horrible kids who wait for the bus. Miss Hopkins, the skinny greaseball who lives downstairs—I feel sorry for her, but she smells bad. But worst of all, there's that retarded person who reels off the numbers of license plates. Zee why cue! Two two oh! He's so gross. He's shaped like a bowling pin."

"That's Ronny. My cousin."

"Your cousin? Oh, David, I'm sorry I said that!"

"In a small town, everybody's related." David was matter of fact. "Poor ol' Ronny's harmless. He lives with two other retarded guys in a halfway house. A social worker brings them food. I check on him, too."

Hetty nodded. She had seen Ronny going in and out of a squat house with false brick siding, just down the street from her. "I'm sorry, anyway. I talk too much. It's just that I feel I can tell you things."

"I like that. You're not factory sealed. Your heart still flips over." He touched her sneakered foot with his own.

The boat bumped on something and Hetty cried out. "Please, let's row back in." Her fear returned. David said nothing but looked almost angry. She tried to joke, "I've always thought, if I drowned, the weirdest things would come back to me, like lost New Year's resolutions."

"It's shallow here, you've got nothing to worry about." But he picked up the oars again. When they reached shore he asked, "What resolutions did you make this year? Do you remember?"

"To never again force a smile or a laugh."

"That's a good thing to decide."

In silence, they tied up the boat.

One day, after a faculty meeting, a harsh rain was falling. The history teacher, Leon Kantz, offered to drive her home, and she accepted, grateful for the dry warmth of his Chevy. Leon Kantz wore his trousers too tight, and she had thought him pompous and arrogant. But they chatted just before the faculty meeting, and she discovered that he had studied in Germany, had played golf in

Scotland. For her benefit, he assumed the proper stance for teeing off and swung an imaginary club. He didn't realize that the meeting had been called to order, and sheepishly he sat down, amid snickers. Hetty grinned at him.

Now, over the thump of the windshield wipers, he said, "Want to go somewhere for a drink?"

"Are there any decent bars around here?"

"No, so we'll make our own." He drove to a liquor store and went in. Hetty watched him from the car. She liked his leather boots and his bull neck and his deep voice, so deep he could be a bass singer in a country and western group. How had she overlooked him before?

It started to snow. Leon slid back into the car and handed her a bottle. "You're the first person I've enjoyed talking to in longer than I can remember, Hetty. You make me want to play."

"We could go to my apartment," she said.

Later, after he was gone, she gazed at herself in the mirror. He had said she was beautiful. She'd had a lover in college who said so too, but she still believed her cheeks were too heavy, her forehead too high. It had happened so fast. She hadn't even looked at the label on the bottle they drank. Well, why should she be ashamed?

Now it was dark, but still early. She wasn't hungry. She sat on her old red sofa, pulling threads in the frayed armrests, her mind blank. The phone rang.

"Hello?"

A breathy whine answered: "I'm watching you. I know you."

In horror, Hetty held the receiver away from her ear, then dropped it back on the cradle. When the phone rang again, she didn't answer, and that night she slept little.

Because the snow was so deep, school was canceled the next day. Hetty passed the morning grading papers, her thoughts snapping back painfully to the phone call and to Leon. I was a fool, she thought, I know nothing about him. By afternoon the day seemed endless. She put on her coat and picked her way down the street to the coffee shop. The snow had stopped, but there were no cars in sight, just a few people wielding shovels. The glare hurt her eyes.

She had drunk two cups of tea before she noticed David Mercer sitting at the counter. He caught her eye in the mirror, winked, and came over.

"You were so lost in thought, I didn't want to disturb you."

"I was just thinking of words," she said hastily. "For a spelling test tomorrow. 'Congratulations' and 'Allegheny' get misspelled all the time."

"Congratulations on your trip to the Allegheny Mountains," and when he laughed, she joined in. "Store's closed," he said. "No business, just this digging out. See my cleared sidewalk? I'm proud of that."

Obediently she looked across the street at his shop.

"Hetty, is something the matter? You look panicky."

"Caffeine does that."

"When I have a problem, I pretend it's somebody else's, so I can be objective. Then I make a list of ways to solve it."

"You're more organized than I am."

"It's people that cause problems. Is somebody upsetting you?"

She shook her head, wishing he would go away, yet not wanting to be alone.

"You won't live here forever," he said. "You'll look back and wonder if you imagined living here." With his fingertip he traced the knuckles on the back of her hand. "But you'll remember the people you met. Even here, there are people to love and hate and feel in-between about. Ambivalence toward somebody can be as permanent a state as love or hate. Ambivalence: put that one on your spelling test."

She gazed down at her empty teacup. When she looked up again, he was gone, striding across the street to his shop, his hands thrust deep into the pockets of his fleecy jacket.

Over the weekend, seized with the desire for change, she bleached her hair from dark blonde to light blonde and painted her nails and lips scarlet. The thought of the long winter ahead filled her with despair. She painted each fingernail to be a little candle to keep the chill away. When the phone rang, she answered it promptly. This time the rasping voice spoke obscene words. Shaken, she slammed it down.

Who? David. Leon. Or a student. Or just a nut. She fell asleep in midafternoon and dreamed that David was tipping her over in the canoe, that she was flailing and drowning in the river. In the dream she heard his cousin Ronny shouting the numbers of license plates. Then she woke and realized he was indeed yelling, right below her window: "Two five nine gee dubya kay!" She put a pillow over her head to drown out the witless monotony of his voice. Exhausted and desperate, she was afraid even to look at the phone. Who was out there wanting to torment her?

The police. Why hadn't she thought of them before? She dialed the non-emergency number. Keep a log, she was told. You can always get your number changed. But it probably won't go on for long. She found herself saying, "Well, it's just been a few times."

She got out a calendar and counted the days until Christmas vacation. But wasn't her teaching contract for a whole year? Over and over she tallied the days until June.

Monday came, and she felt the full impact of the change in her appearance: everyone, from the students to the principal to the janitor, remarked on it. The secretaries and the women teachers buzzed when she passed by, and she grew convinced that they knew what had happened with Leon. Carolyn Foreman tossed her a solid, neutral stare.

Still, she looked for Leon with excitement, and when she found him sitting alone in the lounge, reading a newspaper, she crept up behind him and put her hands over his eyes.

"Guess who."

"I know who," he said, lifting her hands down and kissing the palms. Her heart pounded. As he gripped her hands tighter, she bent down and nuzzled his neck. He stood up and they embraced. He began to play with her breasts; she felt the wonderful pressure of his fingertips through her tight sweater. She was too dizzy to care if someone should come in the door.

"So hot," he whispered. "I've been thinking about you every second. Can I drive you home again?"

"Are you married?"

"Does it matter?"

She had known it in her bones. "No, it doesn't matter."

After school, heading toward her apartment in the dusk, they stopped at a red light. A figure stood on the corner, then crossed the street: David.

Leon made a derisive sound. "There's that weirdo."

"He's a friend of mine!"

Leon turned toward her, frowning. "He was a student of mine, not that long ago. Just a smart-aleck daydreamer. That Woody Woodpecker hairdo. I never liked him."

The light changed, and they lurched forward. Hetty said, "Well, *I* like him."

"A few years ago he tried to start an amateur theater group, but it was no go. He didn't keep at it long enough. He's always talking a big game, but he'll be peddling blue jeans till he drops."

"Don't you think you're being unfair? After all, he's only twenty-five, and how old are you, anyway?" Now she was angry. She wanted to make Leon feel old. "He's one of the few people here who has any ambition. And he has a sense of humor, too."

By the time they reached her apartment, she wanted only to be alone. She jumped out of the car and slammed the door. Leon looked surly. She couldn't believe she'd been attracted to him just a short while before.

What she felt for David was not the same kind of attraction.

She sat at her kitchen table, repairing chips in her red nail polish. The phone rang and she picked it up, her face like stone. It was the voice again, threatening and full of evil. "Hetty Hawken. Your new hair. You're changing, and you like it."

Trembling, she hung up. When she felt better, her thoughts returned to Leon. The next day at lunchtime, she walked from the school to a small downtown apparel shop and bought a set of peach satiny underwear. She and Leon got together that evening, and the next, and the next. They never had much time together, but what time they did have was hungry and desperate and thrilling.

For several weeks her time was absorbed with teaching and with Leon. The phone calls persisted. There was no discernible pattern, and she often let the phone ring unanswered, fearing that grating, half-audible croak. She kept a log with frantic precision, far more carefully than she kept her checkbook or lesson plans. The calls only came when she was alone. She told no one about them.

One evening in December, David invited her over for dinner. Hetty climbed the steps to his apartment over the blue jeans store. Country music was playing on the stereo; she could smell spaghetti. What a relief to be away from her phone! As David set her plate down, he rested his hand on her shoulder.

"Saw you with Leon Kantz." He sat down opposite her at the table, folding his napkin into his lap.

"So? He's a colleague, a friend."

"It's none of my business."

"None at all."

"Oh, Hetty, he's a skirt-chaser! His wife has left him twice, but she always goes back to him. His classes were boring as heck. And he's so vain; I used to see him preening in front of the bathroom mirror."

"Can we talk about something else?" She was tired of defending each to the other, and wondered why she bothered.

"Sure. Just tell me what's the matter."

At the sympathy in his voice, her reserve cracked. She could tell him, couldn't she? "I've been getting these awful phone calls. Obscene, threatening calls. I have no idea who it is."

"Come here." He led her to the sofa. They sat down and he put his arm around her. "How can I help? I have a whistle that would deafen anybody, and a tape recorder—"

"All I want is for the calls to stop!"

"When did they start?"

She took a deep breath. "After Leon first visited me."

"Do you think it's him?"

"I don't think so."

"His wife?"

"I really don't know."

David said softly, "If I could get my hands on anybody who
dared hurt you . . ." Hetty leaned her head against his shoulder
and closed her eyes.

They fell asleep sitting there on the sofa. Hetty woke first. The
country music album had long since ended, and a faint buzz came
from the stereo speakers. David's arm was still around her, and his
face, in repose, was so kind that she hugged him. He woke and
said, "We never ate dinner. It must be cold by now."

Hetty snapped his suspenders. "Now that I'm blonde, I intend
to have more fun."

"Oh, you do?" He kissed her. His lips were gentle, and he
slipped his hands around her waist, then bent down and kicked off
his shoes.

"Now you get rid of your shoes," he said. They laughed de-
lightedly. "Now your socks, and your shirt." When all their clothing was strewn around the living room, they went hand in hand
into the bedroom. It was a long time before they returned to the
table to eat the cold spaghetti.

The next morning David walked her home. The streets were
empty except for Ronny, who was sitting on top of a metal trashcan at the gas station, smoking a cigar, the hood of a tattered
snowsuit pulled over his head. "Zee pee em! Zowie!" He banged
his heels against the trashcan.

The fat man who ran the gas station wiped the windshield of a
car in the service bay. "Shut up!"

Ronny's head whipped around. Uneasy, Hetty stopped, holding
David's arm.

Ronny resumed his litany. "Slow down, dee dee five! That's
from Florida! I like that one!"

The fat man strode toward him and tipped the trashcan, so
Ronny lost his balance and fell forward. "What? Huh?"

"Hey, stupid. Get the hell out of here!" The fat man pointed
down the street, toward where Hetty and David stood. "I'm sick
and tired of you screaming those goddamn numbers! You drive me
crazy! If you stick around much longer, I'll be crazier than you
are!" Gesturing wildly, his face just inches from Ronny's, the fat
man yelled so loud that Hetty's ears rang: "If you ever set foot

here again, I'll have you locked up! Want to go to jail? You can *make* license plates there!''

Stunned, Ronny dropped his cigar, then turned and walked away. The fat man kept yelling, his language violent.

As Ronny came nearer, David raised his hand in greeting, but Ronny lumbered past them blindly, the sleeve of his snowsuit brushing Hetty's arm. David cried, ''Ronny, it's David. It's OK, Ronny.'' But Ronny plunged heedlessly down the sidewalk.

''Want to follow him, or say something to the fat guy?'' Hetty asked. She was unnerved, yet there was another feeling too: catharsis. She had witnessed a venting of rage, and in a way it was glorious.

''No,'' said David. He seemed shaken. He walked Hetty to her door and departed.

There was a note under the door. She unfolded it: Leon wanted to see her that afternoon.

The memory of David's touch swept warmly over her, confusing her. Leon's heavy body and their hurried romps in the dusk seemed distant. She reached over to her coffee table and picked up a navy striped muffler that Leon had left behind. It smelled of Old Spice. No, she wouldn't see him this afternoon; it would be disloyal to David. But why be loyal to anybody? she wondered. What had happened between her and David hadn't been planned, anymore than she'd planned to start with Leon.

I wish Leon weren't married, she thought. I wish David had a college education. But I like them, and they're the best men this town has to offer.

She put the kettle on to boil. Soon it was whistling so loudly that she hardly heard the phone ringing. She raised the receiver to her ear. There was a low chuckle.

''Leon?'' she asked.

Then the voice began again. She couldn't breathe, her hands shook. The voice laughed brokenly.

''Why are you doing this? Who are you?'' she cried.

''You . . . I'm watching you. I know you. I'm coming for you.''

She snatched the cord out of the wall. She was crying.

She packed, hauling her suitcase from the closet and piling

clothes in it, not bothering to remove the wire hangers. She swept her cosmetics into a grocery bag.

There was a knock at the door, then Leon's deep voice: "Hetty? Are you there?"

Wildly, she surveyed the wreck of her closet.

"Hetty, did you get my note? Can I come in?"

Rage overpowered her, and she stormed to the door and wrenched it open. Leon stood there, his wool stretch hat in one hand, a thermos in the other. His eyes widened.

"Hetty, what's the matter?" He stepped toward her.

"Don't you dare come in!" she said, her voice hurting her throat. "I mean it! I'll scream! You're making those calls, aren't you?" She pushed her face close to his, hating him.

"I did call earlier, but your line was busy."

"Calling me, threatening me! Tell me why you did that!"

"I don't know what you mean."

She grabbed his arm, squeezing it, wanting to hurt him. He dropped the thermos, and it went bumping down the steep stairs. His eyes were huge. "Let's go in and talk."

"No! No!" His arm was around her shoulders, and she kicked out at his shins.

"Hetty," he was saying. "Hetty, Hetty!"

Then she heard the foyer door banging open, and rapid footsteps bounding up: David. When he reached her door and saw the two of them there, he paused, catching his breath as if he had run miles.

Leon challenged, "What do you want, David?"

David ignored him, his pale eyes flashing. "Hetty, Ronny hanged himself. He's dead."

He had gone to check on Ronny, he said, and had discovered him with one end of a cord fastened to a light fixture, the other end tight around his neck, and a stepladder kicked out from under him.

"He's dead, and I could have stopped it. That guy was so mad at him this morning, it upset him."

Leon asked, "Have you reported this yet?"

"It was just now that I found him. He was all alone. I got him down and then came here." Tears spurted from David's eyes. Hetty reached out and took his hand. Urgency possessed them all. Hetty's mind said Hurry, hurry—as if hurrying could bring the dead man back to life.

"I'll call the police and have them meet us at Ronny's house," said Leon.

The phone. Hetty watched as he plugged its cord back into the wall. Immediately it began to ring. Hetty said, "I can't bear it. Someone else answer it, but don't say hello when you pick it up."

She grabbed her coat and went downstairs to the cold foyer as the phone shrilled overhead.

The voice. Was she going mad? She could hear it through the walls, could hear it in her head, familiar and knowing: "Hetty, it's happening, Hetty!"

David joined her, frowning.

"David," she whispered, clutching his sleeve.

"I hear it, too."

"Leon?"

"Not Leon." He pulled her close to the door of Miss Hopkins's apartment. The voice was coming from behind the door. David turned the knob but the door was locked. He kicked it open, breaking the wood around the old doorknob, and there was Miss Hopkins, the receiver still in her hand as she whirled toward them.

"It was you! It was your voice!" cried Hetty.

The woman's face was blank. Her mouth opened as if to laugh. "It was a game, Hetty," she said. "You and I played a game, that's all." She pushed her broken door shut in Hetty's face.

Then Leon was coming down the stairs, and together he and Hetty and David went out on the street.

"Why did she do that to me?" Hetty asked, bewilderment and shock washing over her. "I was just her neighbor." David's arm was firmly around her; she felt his warmth through the bulk of their coats.

"Christ," said Leon. "A loon."

"We have to see about Ronny," David said.

The calls will stop now, Hetty thought. She hated and envied me . . . I shouldn't be surprised that she was the one.

"Are you all right?" David asked. He stopped, letting Leon walk on ahead of them. "She's crazy. She zeroed in on you because you're young and pretty and she has nothing to do."

"I'm fine," she said. Ronny's house came in sight, and they ran toward it.

When I get home, Hetty thought, I'll unpack my things and do something nice for David. Dear David. I don't have to be afraid anymore. I came here and didn't like this town and I found two men to enjoy. For that, I got targeted for that awful anger.

It wasn't my fault.

It wasn't.

News from China

Last night I heard my neighbor's cats fighting, sounding like demons, and I did what I always do: stuck my fingers in my ears and prayed. Now it's lunchtime. Mama's cooking a cylinder of frozen meat, scraping the done part off with a spatula. It smells wonderful. I can hear my brother Wayne out in the yard, fooling around with the car. Because it's already running, the old Chevy makes its sick angry sound of protest when Wayne turns the ignition key. Wayne's helpless around machinery, around all mechanical things. Mama and I take care of the fix-its here.

I'm worried about Wayne. He's twenty-four but seems older, old even. The last two years he spent out west, and we hardly ever heard from him. Now he's back, working as a substitute teacher in my high school. I've never had him for a teacher, but I've heard he gives strange punishments to kids who're bad, or just ones he doesn't like. He makes them do push-ups in front of the class. Skip Gregory told me, "Your brother's creepy," and I said, "You wart. You don't want to know what people say about *you*."

But once I did happen to walk by Wayne's classroom, and there on the floor were two girls and a guy, doing push-ups, while Wayne stood stiffly at the blackboard. Counting. "Twenty-two, twenty-three." The boy and one of the girls looked like they planned to get even with Wayne, but the other girl was almost crying. I shuddered and walked by fast.

"Do you want lunch, Wayne?" Mama calls out the back door. "Where's he going, Aleta?"

"Probably the library," I say.

Since he's been home, Wayne has developed an intense friendship with the librarian, Margaret. It's a small library, and you can almost hear what Wayne and Margaret are saying to each other, because they don't trouble to lower their voices. Margaret wears her hair real short, razor cut. Her dresses are full and flowery and she wears sandals way into the cold part of fall. All her features push together in the middle of her face. For a while she played a stereo in the library, telling people that a low level of music improved concentration, that all the big city libraries played music. Besides, she said, she hated silence. But people complained, so she had to put the stereo away.

Once I asked Wayne, "Why don't you ask Margaret out?" He tightened his lips and looked sideways down at me from his immense height.

"Margaret's just a friend," he said.

"What do you talk about?"

"Books. Well, that's what I talk about. Margaret really doesn't like to read."

Mama and I hear the Chevy chug away, trailing azure smoke down the short driveway into the unpaved alley. A cat streaks out of the way. Wayne drives too fast for the alley.

I pour a glass of milk for Mama and one for me, and we take our plates to the table. Mama sighs.

"This may sound hard to believe," she says, "but sometimes I think Wayne would be different if only I'd given him a different name. You were easy to name. Your daddy named you after the queen in his favorite comic strip, 'Prince Valiant.' But your brother? Even when he was little, I thought about giving him a legal name change as a present. Now it's too late." She frowns through the window. "Wayne."

After lunch I go next door to the Herrolds'. They're going on vacation and have asked me to look after their cats, take in the mail, and water the plants. They're young, just a few years older than Wayne, but he seems far older.

Joyce Herrold opens the door. I'm always surprised by how tiny she is. She must weigh about ninety pounds. Her long hair is knotted up in a sweaty little bun, and she looks like a child in her old nylon sundress. Wayne doesn't like the Herrolds because he once saw Joyce wearing her bathing suit to cut grass, and he said she was cheap.

Joyce invites me in. Her kitchen's nifty—big baskets, the expensive split-oak kind, sit on top of the high cabinets, and lots of glazed copper pots hang from hooks on the walls.

"Here they are!" cries Joyce, swooping down to scoop up a tabby cat and a black one. Like a magician, she plucks a white kitten from behind her neck, rattling off their names so fast I'll never remember them.

"How much should I feed them, Joyce?"

"Six cans a day, plus crunchies." She brandishes a bag of cat chow. Her butcherblock counter is stacked with dozens of cans.

I follow her into the living room to see where the plants are. The furniture is gorgeous. Her curio cabinet holds more silver than the downtown jewelry store does. The rugs have crazy Oriental patterns. Where can you even buy rugs like that? I've never seen them in stores.

"I'm not very good with plants," I say.

"Whatever you do will be fine." She snaps a dead leaf off a coleus. "But promise me something, Aleta!"

"What?" I ask, alarmed.

"That you'll play with my angels!" She lifts the tabby to her face and kisses both sides of its whiskers. She shuts her eyes and holds the animal close,and for a moment I'm afraid she'll cry. "Play with them and make sure their water is fresh. I don't know if I can stand to be away from them all week."

After I leave, I think about all the things that could go wrong while I'm in charge. The cats and Joyce have made me nervous. I feel certain the cats are able to talk to Joyce, to truly speak to her. When she returns, they'll tell her I tormented them. Joyce will listen with horror, pressing their triangular faces to her own, weeping. And she'll fly at me in a vengeful fury.

At dinner I describe Joyce's beautiful house to Mama and Wayne. "There's a big glassfront cabinet with silver and china in it. One shelf is just for silver ice buckets. She has special little pieces of paper she hides in the corners so the silver won't tarnish."

Wayne slams down his fork. "Some people just have too much."

Mama says, "Now, Wayne! You can't hold it against them if they happen to have things. Her husband works hard."

Mama has a job with the phone company, and we have some benefits from Dad's life insurance. He died ten years ago. I used to work part-time at a fast-food place, but I hated it and left, and now I'm trying to get a housepainting job, which would pay great money, especially for a sixteen year old. I wonder what Wayne is doing with the money he makes. Substitute teachers do OK. Always, after their salaries are printed in the paper, people get mad and write letters to the editor, saying the school board pays substitutes too much.

For a while we eat in silence. Wayne's folding chair creaks, as if it's too angry to speak. At last Wayne says, "I have begun something important today."

"What?" Mama and I ask together. Mama's eyes look fearful, hopeful. Wayne seems pleased to have grabbed our attention.

"See all those books I brought home from the library?" He gestures to a pile of dusty hardbacks. "I'm going to choose a new religion. I'm going to read about many religions and then decide which one I want to be."

"Which religion is Margaret?" I ask. Wayne blinks.

"As a matter of fact, Margaret is still deciding, too."

"May I read the books?" Somehow, I don't believe there's text inside, or even pages. If I open the covers, something will jump out and punch me in the nose.

"When I'm through," says Wayne. He sounds the way he used to sound when we were little and I was trying to get the funnies away from him. Now it's hard to believe he ever read the funnies.

The next day is Sunday. Mama feels tired and says for Wayne and me to go ahead to church without her. "Is this your last day as a Baptist, Wayne?" she asks.

"Just my first day as a truly questioning individual," he answers, and Mama brightens. She wants him to be happy.

But somehow, on the way to church, as I stride rapidly to keep up with Wayne, I'm uneasy. His black suit must have extra padding in the shoulders, because he looks powerful in it, even though really he's thin. He's talking more than he's talked in ages, all about our preacher and how he can't stand him.

"He's using religion to further his own ends. He has the congregation totally hoodwinked, the fools."

"Old Reverend Gates? He's boring, Wayne, but he's not trying to doublecross anybody! Not everybody likes him, but—"

"Then why don't they band together and get rid of him?"

I laugh, picturing Wayne hoisting Reverend Gates onto a ducking stool in front of a rampaging mob. The image becomes chilling and I stop laughing.

We're late, and we slide into a back pew during a hymn. Wayne holds the hymnbook at chest level but stares at the backs of the people ahead of us. I try to remember when Wayne started being real serious in church. Way back in my mind is one Sunday when we played a game with the titles of hymns, whispering "between the sheets" after them. " 'At Last I Have Found Paradise'—between the sheets." " 'Gladly to Follow Thee'—between the sheets." At the time, I didn't really understand the game. But Wayne was about fourteen then, and he seemed to have a crush on a girl in his Sunday school class. Then he started being real serious about church.

I think hard about Margaret. Her selection of books in the library strikes me as odd. Lots of how-to books—how to make your own home repairs, how to train dogs. So is she practical? And she has loads of silly romances. One series is all about nurses—*Jungle Nurse*, *Desert Nurse*, *High-Rise Nurse*—in which the nurses are all pursued by dashing, relentless doctors. So maybe Margaret's very romantic. But she just doesn't seem to *like* books. Once, for an English assignment, I asked for *Moby Dick*.

"Never heard of it," she told me. And she meant it.

Now, whenever I see her wheeling a cartful of books onto the little dumbwaiter that lifts them up to the mezzanine, I imagine she's really dumping the books down in the basement, to go out with the trash. Then I recall Wayne's stack of books on religion.

Margaret must have helped pick them out.

I tune in on Reverend Gates. He's making his little preamble of announcements, a preamble that stretches into what is supposed to be sermon time, but nobody minds. He announces who's been sick, who's had a baby, and which activities will take place this week.

"Next Sunday," says Reverend Gates, "I'll be away at the district conference, but our own Mr. Bill Owens will act as lay preacher."

Suddenly Wayne is on his feet. Startled, I stare up at him. His face is paper white, and he opens his mouth to speak.

"Yes," he says loudly, coldly. At the sound of that one word, the entire congregation spins around in the pews. "Yes, we'll play church again next Sunday, as we are doing right now. Someone will be here to help us play church next Sunday." He swings his head in an arc, as if looking at each face in the room. Then he sits down.

The organ falters into a hymn. I sit frozen, Wayne's words echoing sickly above the music. A current of shock buzzes among the pews. Reverend Gates's face is slack, dumbfounded. Beside me, Wayne breathes hard through his nostrils, the breath making squeaky, windy noises.

As soon as the hour ends, I pull on his arm. "Come *on*." He rises, and we're the first ones out the door. I can't look Reverend Gates in the eye. He'll think I, too, hate him, but I can't worry about that now. I'm glad Mama wasn't here today, as glad about that as I am mad at Wayne.

When we're safely out on the sidewalk, out in the coppery sunshine of a fine fall day, I turn on him. "Why in hell did you do that?"

Calmly, he says, "Because I wanted to be the lay preacher next Sunday. I actually offered to do it. But no, the choice of the myopic Gates was Bill Owens, who has about as much spirituality as a turnip."

"But Wayne, do you have any experience as a minister? I thought you were a teacher when you were out west."

"I was many things out west, and I'm still all of those things."

I could shake him. We stand there under a maple tree, its leaves a luminous Crayola orange. "You're always thinking about yourself. You're selfish and weird, and I refuse to go to church with you anymore. But you better tell Mama what you did today, because I don't want her to hear it from somebody else."

I turn and stride away from him. When I look back, he's still standing under the tree, its leaves brushing the top of his hair. I'm too upset to face Mama right away, and besides, it's feeding time for Joyce's cats.

I take my spare key and let myself into the Herrolds' house. It's cool and dim, smelling of floor wax. The tabby and the black cat spring out of thin air. I have to hunt for the white kitten. There it is, under the TV set. I feed them and let tap water run into a big plastic pitcher to water the plants.

With Wayne's words still blasting in my ears, I ask the cats what I should do about him. I'm beginning to think Mama can't do anything about him. After all, he's a grown man. I find myself hoping he'll leave again. I don't really know what made him leave before, or what made him come back. All I know is that he left after college, which seemed like a natural enough time to leave home. When he called to say he was coming back, I hoped he'd have had some good adventures that would make him happy and fun to be around.

Gagging, I clean out the litter box. Joyce, I know, would not have gagged, out of sheer pride. When I'm through, I pick up each cat in turn. Their ears flatten and swivel to the side. From now on, I'll be a cat around Wayne, listening better than I have before.

The phone rings at seven, which means Wayne has work for the day. I realize he's gotten fewer calls in recent weeks than he was getting back in September, when he was first hired. Wayne and I eat our cereal in the still kitchen, which smells musty from last night's rain. I love fall.

"What class will you teach today, Wayne?"

"World Cultures, for Mrs. Peabody."

"That's one of mine." Dread displaces the Special K in my stomach. What if he makes somebody do push-ups? I couldn't stand it. For a minute I consider staying home, but then I remember that I have to watch him. "It's easy. I'll show you what we're doing today." I reach for the textbook and hold it unopened with its spine against the table.

"Well?"

"Wayne," I begin. I've practiced the words to myself in the shower, but getting them out is hard. I try to sound as matter of fact as Ann Landers. "Wayne, I've noticed you seem angry these days. I'm not criticizing you. But I wonder if you'd feel better if you went to a counselor to get these feelings out of your system. The counselor at school is real nice. You could go to him free."

There. The words are out.

I stare down at my thumbs, the nails just touching over the white closed pages of the book. The silence stretches out from the table to the ceiling, a hard, blank silence stirred only by the pulse in my ears. When I finally look up at Wayne, he's regarding me as if he's just discovered a few bad flakes in his cereal. He drains his glass of juice and motions toward the book. "Show me which chapter you're on."

I'm furious. "Just tell me one thing. Have you told Mama what you did in church?"

"As a matter of fact, yes."

"Fine. See you in class." I shove the book into his hands and go.

All day I wait for reports of push-ups, but none come. It seems Wayne is simply following the lesson plan. Still, when I walk into his classroom—my last class of the day—I'm frightened for him and for myself. I can't believe he's my brother, this sour, strange person. Was he ever fun? When he begins class, "My name is Mr. Snyder," everybody looks at me. My heart beats in my ears like a helicopter.

"Today, for this class only, I have a special guest," he announces, as if he's a talk show host. When I snap my head up from the desk, lo and behold: there's Margaret.

She must have been sitting in the back of the room. Her bra shows through her thin, India-cotton dress, a flowing gunmetal garment stamped with gold leaves, bunchy around her big hips. Calluses show on her heels as she walks over to stand next to Wayne. She's wearing Ben Franklin glasses midway down her nose, and she and Wayne exchange expressions of triumph.

Grasping a stub of chalk, Wayne scrawls "Margaret Conlee" on the blackboard. "As most of you know," he says, "Miss Conlee is the community librarian. She not only knows books, she has traveled widely." Margaret stands rigidly at Wayne's side, and kids snicker. Margaret searches out the gigglers with her small eyes and stares them down. "Today, she will bring us up to date on the current situation of China, where she visited last year."

Wayne retreats to the back of the classroom; I hear him knock into a chair as he sits down.

"Yes, last year I visited China," says Margaret, "and I'd give my right ass to go back." She slaps her behind. "It's very poor there; we're talking huts. You people, with cars that your parents give you and the jeans that cost a week's pay from McDonald's, you don't know what it's like to swat a thousand flies off the meat you'll eat for supper. The government, of course, is trying to raise the level of prosperity, but it's slow going. The people farm with plows and oxen. China has billions of people and many can't read or write. I did visit a few libraries. They're only allowed to have certain books. A lot of the oldest works have been lost or destroyed, and anti-government books are banned. Still, the government is within its rights to try and equalize the goods and services that are available. That's more important than books. I walked on the Great Wall."

How old is she? I try to estimate. She tosses me a focused frown as she describes Chinese airplanes—"rickety buckets," she says, "unsafe for takeoff, flight, and landing, rocketing along with windows open and passengers screaming with fear."

I'd had no idea she'd been to China. As I listen to her and watch her, I grow convinced that she is Wayne's destiny. She can put into words the anger that seethes inside him. I see them as missionaries, saving the soul of China. Boldly, I swivel around in my seat, hoping to find Wayne mesmerized by her. Instead he's gazing out the window. I wish he were handsomer. Like me, he has a long lantern jaw. But maybe Margaret prizes his homeliness.

"In China, premarital sex is taboo. Not like here! And for married couples, affairs mean ostracism by the community. Monogamy is strictly observed. Religion is officially banned, but some people still worship in secret."

When the bell rings, I'm aware how quickly time has passed. The class hurries out the door and I follow, casting a backward glance at Wayne and Margaret remaining behind in the empty room. I think, Good. I wait outside the door, the end-of-day stampede whirling past me.

Suddenly Margaret hurtles out of the room, slamming the big slab of a door behind her. Her dirty heels pound down the hallway and she vanishes.

I push the door open. Wayne is lingering behind his desk, flipping the pages of a daytimer.

"What happened, Wayne?"

He continues to turn the pages. Finally: "Margaret just about wasted everybody's time, and I told her so. I had asked her to talk about the Chinese system of government and its benevolent effect on the people, but instead she talked about airplanes and silly details. She was altogether the travelogue-ist. In all of our previous conversations she has been abstract, yet precise."

"But she was wonderful! You're lucky to have her as a friend. Have you ever quarreled with her before?"

"It wasn't a quarrel. I'm merely disappointed."

"She did you a favor, Wayne! This was the best class all year."

He takes a pencil, places it between his teeth, and turns another page. I sneeze. It must be the chalk dust. I sneeze again, and again. When I leave, Wayne is still hunched over the desk.

By suppertime, my throat aches searingly. Mama fixes me a hot lemonade as Wayne picks at his pork chops. He makes notations in a little spiral-bound notebook.

"What's that?" Mama asks him.

"Margaret's phone number," I say. This cold makes me feel mean: I want to put Wayne on dangerous ground.

"I'm adding up my salary," he says. "I was fired at lunch-time today, but they let me finish out the day. The principal didn't like it that I made people do push-ups, and he won't be calling anymore."

"I'm sorry," says Mama.

But I'm glad. It serves him right.

To his pork chops, Wayne says, "I had better look elsewhere. I don't plan to be here much longer."

When Mama leaves for her church circle meeting, I lie down on the sofa. Once I'm lying down, I don't think I can ever get up again. My head feels thick and dumb. But I want to pin Wayne down. "So where do you plan on going next?"

Sheltered behind his newspaper, he doesn't answer.

"When I go to college," I say, "I hope I get a roommate like Margaret. I bet she galvanized a lot of people into campus causes, in her time."

He says nothing.

I go on, "The reason she likes you so much is, she senses you're a fellow troublemaker. She likes your radical fire. Have you decided on a new religion yet?"

"Isn't it time you fed those cats next door?"

I have forgotten the cats. They must be hungry. I sit up, but my head throbs miserably. "Wayne, could you feed them? I feel terrible."

He holds out his hand, and I toss him the key and sink back on the sofa.

I must have fallen asleep, because I wake with a sense of time having passed. Why isn't Wayne back yet? I picture him robbing the Herrolds' house, sweeping all of the silver off the shelves of the curio cabinet with one motion of his superlong arm, thrusting flatware and ice buckets into a burlap sack to give to the poor. Or to keep: I'm never sure whether his resentment of other people's prosperity is on behalf of have nots in general or simply for himself. Suppose he does rob them. What would I tell Joyce?

I sit up and drag myself to the window. A downstairs light is flaring over at the Herrolds'. Maybe Wayne has realized how silly he acted toward Margaret; maybe he called her and invited her to come over and examine the Herrolds' undeserved wealth. Maybe they're setting up a slide projector to view pictures of Margaret stalking along the Great Wall. I imagine that they will then head upstairs, only to have the Herrolds arrive home early, rousting Margaret and Wayne from violent activity.

The cats. He must not let them out. If they get out, they'll fight the other cats in the neighborhood. I have to tell him. I start out the door. It's colder than I'd expected, a frosty chill that clears my stuffy head. I squeeze through the hedge that separates our yards. But instead of going straight to the door, I make my way toward the window of the lighted room.

I'm scared, and I don't know why. So often I've felt Wayne watching me, felt indignant at his cold staring observation, as if I'm a stinging insect that threatens him, or an ice cube on the floor that he might slip on. I've grown into the habit of giving him his privacy. I've wanted to help him, and I've wanted to hurt him with words. But I've never watched him through a window before, like this, and I don't know if I should do so now.

What am I afraid of? Do I expect to see him in one of Joyce's dresses, combing his eyelashes?

On tiptoe, I strain to reach the window, high off the moist ground. The shade is pulled nearly all the way down, but a two-inch strip of viewing space remains at the bottom.

There's Wayne, sitting on a tufted leather sofa, holding a cat on his lap, stroking its fur slowly. Another cat lies curled beside him. His long legs are crossed at the knee, as formally as if he were awaiting an interview.

He must have been sitting there for a long time.

I ease down off my toes and lean against the side of the house, my palms flat against the clapboard walls. For so long I've raged against him because he's cold to Mama and me. I don't understand his way of being alone. Ever since he came home, and even long before that, I've thought of him as a kind of code, something I could decipher and understand. He makes all of my days feel like hair parted on the wrong side. It may be that I can try to like him all my life, without succeeding. I recall how, when he was little, he'd give the same answer to any question: "Yes, no, and maybe so." He hasn't changed very much, at all.

Stick my fingers in my ears and pray: that's what I do when I hear Joyce's cats fighting, deep in the night. More or less, it may be all I can do for Wayne.

I duck through the hedge to my own yard, my own house, leaving him undisturbed, over there.

Yard Sale

Oliver was in charge of bringing customers in, and it was a grand feeling. Up and down the street he went, round and round the block, yelling, "Yard sale! *Eeeyarrrd sale!*" so loudly that in the middle of "yard," as he burred over the *r* and came down hard on the *d*, his ears buzzed and he could barely hear himself at all. Every time he saw somebody on the sidewalk, he ran up and told about the sale: "At my house! 306 Walnut Street. Loads of stuff!" But nobody came. Glumly his mother and father, Mr. and Mrs. McShane, stood on the porch with their arms folded across their chests and their hands tucked under their armpits. They rearranged the pots and pans on the card table, jerked at the rack of old clothes, changed a price sticker here and there, and plumped down in the broken armchair to knock the dust out of its big soft cushion. Nobody came.

People even crossed the street to avoid the sale, but mostly the sidewalks were empty. The heat had driven people inside.

Next door to the McShanes, Mary Flagg was thinking about her life so far. Her second-story sleeping porch contained a folding cot, a rocking chair where she sat, and a white wicker stand that held a pitcher of very sweet iced tea and a box of day-old glazed doughnuts. Her hands trailed sugar down the paper as she made a list of all the people she had ever known. Now and then she spoke to her cat: "The weather keeps thinking up new ways to be mean . . . Fleas know just where to bite, under the elastic of your underwear . . . Next week I'm getting married!" Her cat only curled his front feet under his chest and looked critical.

The breeze cooled Mary's face. She set aside the pages of names she had listed so far and began to write on a fresh sheet of paper. The list had over three hundred names on it, which meant she'd gotten as far as fifth grade. It included relatives, all of whom she had met early in life and some of whom now lay in their graves.

"Why'm I doing this?" But it was what she'd always wanted to do, and who could tell? Once she was married she'd have all sorts of things to tend to and this might be her very last chance to make this list. She wanted to remember, Lord, everybody she'd ever known or met or even seen. Names had always been easy for her. She closed her eyes and pictured her sixth-grade classroom; she could recall where everybody sat. She opened her eyes and poked her pencil into her curls. Before she'd thought of making the list, she'd been practicing wedding hairdos. Now her scalp itched from hairspray, and the elaborate waves hung over her shoulders and halfway down her back. The little topknot on her crown was wilting. She bit into another doughnut. Here she was, twenty-five, and life was sweet as a dream.

Except for Oliver. So noisy! Leaning forward in her rocking chair, she looked straight down into the McShanes' yard. Mr. McShane was picking his nose, Mrs. McShane dropped a hairdryer— the heavy old domed salon-style kind that nobody would ever buy—and then searched in the high, starved grass for the loose screws and sprockets that had fallen out of it.

Weslee and I will never be like that, Mary vowed. She told the cat, "If we had a yard sale, things'd sell."

"*Eeeeyarrdd saaale!*" Oliver cried from across the street. He had his summer haircut. His shadow stuck to his feet on the hot sidewalk like a basketball that had melted while he dribbled it. Looking up, he saw Mary, who had tipped forward in her rocking chair and braced herself in the open window with her arms.

"Come to our yard sale!"

"But I have everything I need," said Mary, "and I'm getting married in a few days. I want to travel light."

"Don't you need some furniture?" Oliver persisted.

Oliver's mother said, "Go over to Isabella Street, son! Find people! What are we going to do with all this junk?"

Five hundred, Mary exulted. I'm up to five hundred people. Mother and father and sister and brothers (one alive and one dead when he was still little) and aunts, uncles, cousins, grandparents, great-grandma, family friends, the people who'd come to their parties, her classmates and teachers, all the other people who'd worked at the school, all the neighbors in every place she'd ever lived, the lady who used to sew clothes for her, the egg man, the bad friend of her cousins, the children at the orphanage she'd visited one time, the Santa Claus who led the Christmas parade, everybody at the church she'd gone to when she was little, people she'd met on vacation, store clerks, waiters, hairdressers, people who'd come to shake her hand so she'd vote for them, her boyfriends, their families—oh, it would take a long time. And that would bring her only a little way in her life. If she couldn't remember a name, she wrote a description.

She wanted to remember everybody, because she had moved around enough in her life to realize what staying in one place and getting to know people was supposed to mean. She had lived in the south and in the north and for a little while even in the west, and now she was home in Virginia with no plans to ever leave it. This little town—this little town was just fine. She made stained-glass windows and sold them to people who liked beautiful things. She'd made the windows for three years since getting out of college, and she'd traveled around to see places. Now she was back in Virginia, living in a tiny town that smelled always of its famous hams.

Six months ago, things had changed. It was in the winter, when she'd gone up to Richmond to do some shopping. That was how she'd met Weslee, when she was looking for a fallen glove in a downtown parking lot.

Getting married in a week. They weren't going to make a big deal of it. In a few days she'd go to her parents' house in the mountains for the wedding. It would be small. Now every morning her mother called to say, "Mary? Don't you think you'd better get in your car and drive on up right now? Your wedding's so soon!"

and she'd say, "In a few days." Yes, it would be soon. Her land-
lady had already rented the house to somebody else. Weslee had a
big house in the Fan District of Richmond. It had so many windows that at night, with the lights all lit up, it had its own great
big smile. The house was guarded by burly blue spruce trees. And
that house would be her house. She didn't want to move anymore.
She'd told Weslee: "If I move in, I'm never moving out."

Weslee: his shoulders shook hard when he laughed. He called
her sweetheart. When she'd worked through her memory for all
the people she had ever known, she would finally come to his
name, and then she'd stop. His would be the last name on the list.

Across the street from Mary, one of her neighbors envied her
the breeze that blew into her sunporch. His own apartment—three
rooms rented on the upper floor of an old Victorian—was gunshot-
level with Mary's sleeping porch. But Bushrod Keller didn't have
a porch, just a chair and an electric fan pulled close to the window. He longed for the sepulchral, cave-like chill of his movie
theater, but he'd hurt his leg and could hardly walk. He was always hurting himself, bruising his heavy arms and legs while doing the simplest things, working on the film machinery, straining
his back lifting the heavy projector into place. Then yesterday
he'd slipped on a pile of ice cubes that somebody had dumped out
of a soft drink. He'd been chugging down the aisle and fell, twisting his knee. A few kids laughed at him. It was just before the
matinee. By the time the movie was over, his ankle had swollen
so that he had to drive home with his left foot.

Worst of all, his assistant had left town without even giving notice, so today, a precious business day, the theater was closed. Not
that too many people would show up, a scant handful in the
evening. But still.

Bushrod had loved Mary for so long that it was a habit, like
going to work. Oh yes, she was friendly, waving her hand when
she saw him from across the street. Greeting him at the theater
when her boyfriend came to take her out. The boyfriend, a hard-
looking man with dark temples and rapid speech, never seemed to
remember Bushrod, but was ready to tell him how to run his busi-

ness: "You ought to show some foreign films. Have an oldies festival." Bushrod would say, "Maybe sometime." But if Mary had said that about foreign films, he would have rushed to his catalogs and ordered a bunch.

Movies had taught him so much about human nature, at least in theory, so why were people so hard to figure out in actual practice? He knew he was a fat man, not attractive to women, least of all to someone like Mary. He had loved her for so long that the love had gone through all sorts of stages: devotion, infatuation, irritation. In reality, he never got past the "Hi." There would never be a movie based on that, the fact that he lived across the street from her and loved her and only said hi.

He had figured she would marry her boyfriend sooner or later, but when he heard her tell Oliver, "In a few days," he felt sick. So it was too late. Too late to lose weight, become handsome, grow bold. She would never belong to him, and soon there'd come a day when he saw her for the last time. All his life, it had been too late.

And that letter. The letter on his bureau. Painfully, he pushed himself up from his chair, limped across the room, and picked it up from the clutter of brushes, hair tonic, loose change, bills, and rolls of movie tickets. A letter from Heidi.

Heidi was a girl, or woman, that he'd met at a church revival earlier in the summer. She was prissy and always talking about Jesus. He knew it wasn't fair to think about her like that, because after all, wasn't Jesus the right reason to go to a revival? It was a sticky night in June when they met. He'd felt lonely after the movie theater emptied out, and he drove out into the country to think about Mary. It was late, the moon was high and little and the lightning bugs had all shut down for the night. He passed by this tiny church he'd hardly noticed before, and there was a tent all set up, glowing yellow with lights. He nosed his car up softly, hardly crunching on the gravel.

He never saw the preacher, but he heard his words pouring forth through the thick crowd of men and women and children who rocked on benches trying to get a better view. People made room for Bushrod at the edge of the tent and he heard the preacher reading from Hosea: "For they sow the wind, and they shall reap the whirlwind. The standing grain has no heads, it shall yield no meal; if it were to yield, aliens would devour it . . ."

Mary, Mary. The powerful words expressed his feelings about her. He covered his face with his hands, then felt an insistent tap on his shoulder.

Before he knew it, he was sharing a Bible with a girl who smelled of witch hazel, who whispered her name and wrote her phone number on a page of Ecclesiastes.

Mary's phone rang. Bushrod heard it, of course; the street was so quiet he could just about hear the sidewalks expanding in the heat. Mary vanished into her house. For some moments, Bushrod gazed at her empty sleeping porch. If only he could talk to her before she got married. If only she would change her mind and never leave.

"Mary, it's time you went on home!" Weslee said, his voice just a little melody on the phone. "Your mama called me and said what's going on? Said Mary hasn't come home and won't say when. Mary, your mama's ready to bake the cake."

"Uh-huh, a sixty-three egg cake, all white and the prettiest cake you ever saw. It's a hundred-year-old recipe."

"Won't it be too big? That sounds like a great big cake."

"It'll be just the right size."

While Mary talked, she looked over to the McShanes' yard and noticed that they were taking the yard sale down.

"Call the Salvation Army," Mrs. McShane snapped to her husband. "They'll come and get this stuff."

Up in Richmond, Weslee hung up on Mary, a sudden *click* that signaled his exasperation. Mary was the key to his life. He'd grown up as a tough kid, his parents smoked and drank along with him. But he'd always worked hard, put himself through college, and now he ran this big beautiful department store and had a house so grand his eyes filled with tears whenever he looked at it. The house was meant to belong to Mary, too.

Sixty-three eggs? He felt sick.

Mary picked her way through the McShanes' small yard, her nose sharp to the scent of used clothes and tired furniture. How similar people's lives seemed when revealed through their discarded possessions. This could be any of a hundred million families.

"How much is this coffee pot?" she asked Mrs. McShane.

"Two smackers."

"That's too much." Mary put it down. "It's broken."

"For some people, anything's too much."

Her cheeks burning, Mary retreated to her house. What a witch! She wouldn't miss the McShanes.

A deliveryman was at her door with a package. She signed for it, took it inside, opened it up: a hummingbird feeder.

"I didn't order this," she said aloud.

She checked the address. It wasn't meant for her at all. Who lived at 309 1/2? She squinted across the street. Bushrod, of course! Bushrod Keller.

She crossed the street with the package under her arm. The sky was a burning silver plate over the world. In a moment she was in the apartment house, bounding up the stairs, knocking on his door.

Bushrod saw her coming. He panicked, yanking the door open after Mary's knuckles had barely touched it.

"Bushrod! Hi. Did you order a hummingbird feeder?"

"What?"

"The deliveryman brought this. I think it's yours."

"Oh, yes. Thank you!" He took it from her, frantically trying to calibrate his response. He was conscious of the messiness of the room, its Ben-Gay odor. Mary was smiling. "Would you like to come in?" he asked.

He proffered his window chair, and she sank into it. She was here, she was really here. His mind was a desert, a sheet of ice. Should he offer her a drink? Of what?

"You're limping, Bushrod!"

"I hurt my ankle at work." He set the hummingbird feeder on his bureau.

"Can I help you with anything—ice, aspirin? Does it hurt?"

That was how he knew she'd be: kind. That was what you looked for all your life, somebody to really care if your ankle hurt. He relaxed. "I can get around," he said. But he was afraid his bare swollen ankle looked ugly to her.

He just stared at her as she sat in his oversized chair looking, in her pink dress, like a petal that had fallen through his window. He could never say what was in his heart.

"I heard you tell Oliver you're getting married, Mary."

"That's right."

He fired staple questions at her as if she were a bride in a survey: Was she excited about her wedding? Where would she go on her honeymoon? Would she keep her maiden name? "It's such a pretty name," he said. "Mary Flagg."

"No, I'll take Weslee's name. I'll be Mary Turner then."

"Oh."

She reached out the window and touched a tree limb. "Is this where you're going to hang that feeder? I think that's a wonderful, imaginative thing to do." She drew her head back in. "Could you do me a favor, Bushrod?"

"I would be honored."

"Take care of my cat when I go? Cats don't like to move. If you could just start feeding him, he'll be yours."

"I like cats. I'll take good care of him."

Mary got up from the chair. "Thank you. Are you sure you don't want an icepack for that ankle?"

He shook his head.

"Goodbye, Bushrod," she said from the doorway.

"I'll miss you, Mary."

"Thank you." She looked him full in the face, and then she was gone.

Until the sun changed position on the walls of his room, he sat in the big armchair and replayed the scene again and again in his mind. He was happy. He would keep on loving her, and the love would continue to change and go through phases, even if he didn't see her for a long time. He was happy enough to fetch the letter from Heidi on his dresser and write a passionate reply.

A long, low station wagon pulled up beside the McShanes' house, and a man got out. He was short and very blond, with a face that looked like he'd come out of a hundred foster homes with a good sense of humor. A green tattoo decorated each arm. Oliver greeted him from a seat in a persimmon tree: "Hey."

"Salvation Army. You folks got some stuff for me?"

"*Mom! Dad!*" Oliver yelped. "He's here!"

After her visit with Bushrod, Mary had just had time to make herself a Coke with lots of chipped ice. Her kitchen was stifling, and she felt lazy. She went outside to watch the McShanes load their things into the station wagon.

Wait a minute. That driver seemed familiar. She looked closer. Number one hundred seventy-one on her list, wasn't it? Bobby Eubanks? Yes, she remembered him from the fourth grade.

"Bobby!" she said.

"Mary? Mary Flagg! Well, I think I'll kick up my heels with joy. How did you end up in this town?"

"Because I'd lived just about everywhere else."

She gave him a sip of her Coke. Mrs. McShane shoved the big hairdryer into the station wagon, and Bobby Eubanks said, "Sorry, ma'am, we can't take that. We can't even *give* those big hairdryers away."

"So even the Salvation Army's turned picky. I swear I'll never give a yard sale again." Mrs. McShane jerked the hairdryer out of the car and dumped it on the grass.

"Want to go for a ride, Mary, on this beautiful day?"

"Bobby, I want some Silver Queen corn."

"I know where we can get some." He held open the door for her, and she handed her Coke to Oliver and got in. "Aren't you going to lock your door or get your pocketbook or anything?"

"Nope." Mary rolled down her window. She liked it that he thought it was a beautiful day. Really it was awful, hotter than ever. "I'm sorry you didn't have better luck," she said to the Mc-Shanes.

Bobby Eubanks took the last bag of clothing from Mr. McShane and tossed it into the car, and he and Mary rode off down the street. Oliver hoisted himself back up the persimmon tree. A wind started up, and the sky turned thick-and-thin like old-fashioned gray wool. The wind blew up and down the street and in and around the open windows of the houses, bringing a piece of paper flying out of Mary's sleeping porch and right over to the tree where Oliver was. He climbed down, picked it up, and took it to his mother.

"A list of people to invite to her wedding, I guess. But wait, I happen to know that some of these people are dead! Dead relatives! She's crazy, son. And cheap—wouldn't even spend two bucks on that coffee pot."

"It's broken, anybody can see that."

Was his mother smiling or frowning? Her expression was fierce. She shook the list in her red hand. "I'm glad *my* name isn't on here. She's out of her mind!"

Weslee's sports car took up all the space in Mary's short driveway. He was tired, having driven down from Richmond at the end of a day when every customer in his store seemed to have gone mad. He'd take Mary out to dinner and then they'd go to that goofy little theater and see a flick. At least it'd be cool in there.

"Mary?" He knocked, then saw the door was open. "Mary?"

No answer. He went all through the house. The cat wound between his legs, making it hard to walk. He went upstairs, thinking she was asleep or in the shower.

The list lay in pieces all over the floor of the sleeping porch. Weslee picked it up and scanned it, shaking his head and smiling. But why wasn't his name on any of these pages? He plucked a doughnut from the open box and bit into it.

He went out again. The "Yard Sale" sign was still up at the McShanes'. He saw something sitting on the grass, like a big pale-blue shoulder: a hairdryer, the old-fashioned salon style. An idea hit him. It would be perfect for Mary's long hair. His house in Richmond had space for everything.

"How much you want for this?" he asked the boy up in the tree.

Mary and Bobby pulled over to one roadside stand after another in their search for Silver Queen corn. They bought peaches, snaps, jars of honey, bags of squash, but there was no Silver Queen to be had. The summer'd been too dry, they were told.

"But no other kind will do," said Mary.

As Bobby drove, Mary reached behind her and went through the McShanes' old clothes. She found a motheaten Spanish-looking mantilla and pulled it around her shoulders. She clapped a green fedora onto Bobby's head. Driving along the swerving roads, with their deep forest smell, and with the color and scent of the purchased vegetables all around her, Mary wished she could stay where she was, forever.

But she couldn't, of course. Sooner or later Bobby would drive her home. A knot began to grow in her heart. Fear. Through the car windows the sky was a batch of scorched grape jelly in a ruined pot. Still it would not rain.

The Spanish mantilla had long trailing streamers, all different colors, which flew about in the air rushing through the open windows. Yes, it felt good to be in motion. All right, all right, she said to herself. I can do it now; I'm taking nothing with me and I left my door unlocked. It's the only way. Everything will be all right. Everything will be fine. Saying it to herself, she believed it, and she began to feel happy, too.

"Did you say something?" Bobby asked.

"I said, would you drive me to the mountains? Would you come to my wedding? I have to get home—my mother's baking the cake."

Back on Mary's street, Bushrod poured Hawaiian punch into the hummingbird feeder, hung it from the branch outside his window, lay down, and dreamed. His dreams had credits at the end, and a lion roared.

Weslee fell asleep with all the lights on in Mary's house. Mary's cat leaped out an open window to do some courting of his own. Mr. and Mrs. McShane nodded off while watching TV.

Only Oliver was awake. He sat at his desk in his small hot room, getting some paperwork done. Having studied Mary's list of names, he had divined exactly what it was. He wanted to make a list like that, a list of everybody he'd ever known. He felt connected to Mary, because she thought the same way he did. Her list impressed him. He put her name at the top of his paper. Then his mother, father, grandparents, Mr. Keller across the street, his friends, his teachers . . . It was a big job. But he knew why he had to do it, why Mary had done it . . . He just had to . . . But it was late and hot and it was getting so hard to stay awake . . .

All that moved on the street were Mary's curtains, up on the sleeping porch. All that moved was time.

Eva's Lover

Hard as I try, I can't remember why he came to the house.

Maybe he came to look at the old Plymouth that my parents always had for sale. The car was an automotive practical joke. Every time we drove it over the railroad tracks, both the hood and the trunk flew up, and often the horn stuck, too, so we careered along in a one-vehicle idiot parade. Lazarus, we called that car. Finally it broke down beyond all hope and had to be junked. So nobody ever bought it.

Why did he come? He wasn't a relative or friend or neighbor . . . Maybe he worked in my father's office downtown and was new. Other office people came out to our house all the time, to eat watermelon and cool off, the heat and combat of a day in Richmond clinging to their limp clothes. And neighbors stopped by, their children invading our big straggly yard while my sister Odette and I perched haughtily on the porch, gulping Crackerjacks and waiting for them to go.

But that man: politely, my father introduced him to my sister and me. "Odette, Shirlie, this is Mr. Prendergast."

Young, plump, humble, he stood before us like Joseph before the wives of Potipher. His square pale face, topped with an uneven crewcut, was an over-roasted marshmallow. And that name! Odette and I exchanged looks of incredulity. It was the funniest name we'd ever heard. The next thing I remember, we were collapsed on the porch swing, hysterical, laughing so hard we were sick. Odette's face scared me: it was purple. I couldn't breathe, my lungs felt as carbonated as Mountain Dew. We could see Mr. Prendergast walking in the watermelon patch with our parents, his white-shirted stomach bobbing in the dusk. Whenever we sobered up, the sight of him set us off again. We tried to say his name, but all that came out was a violent wheeze: "Pren—Pren—" We couldn't believe our luck. Our ever-eager net of mockery had snared a treasure. Gasping, we rolled to the floor.

Hoping to avoid punishment, we went to bed early, but the whippoorwills had hardly quieted down when our parents snapped on the light and reproached us.

"You-all embarrassed us to death," Mama said. "He knew you were laughing at him! It was so rude."

"Shirlie, you're eleven," said Daddy. "Too old to act like that. And Odette, you know better. Don't try to say you were laughing at a joke!"

We knew we'd been bad. And yet . . .

Odette pulled the sheet over her head. "Prendergast," she murmured.

We erupted again. This time our parents capitulated and joined in.

That is the happiest memory of my childhood, and maybe of my life.

Now Odette and I don't tell our ages even to our close friends. But we're still young. We *look* young. She lives three hundred miles away, her clock synchronized with mine so that if her phone rings at seven minutes past the hour, she'll know it's me and not her mother-in-law, her husband, or any of her friends.

"Oh, I'm glad it's you!" she always says. "I don't want to talk to any of *them*."

One day I ask her if she remembers Prendergast. "No," she says. "I don't. How can that be, Shirlie? I remember *everything!*"

"You've got to remember."

"I just don't. I did something bad today, Shirlie. Really awful. I had this new kid I was giving a voice lesson to, and he was so good I told his parents he didn't have any talent and not to waste any more money on him. He's five, Shirlie, and I was jealous of him!"

"So? He was competition. You clocked him out."

"That's how I saw it. I feel better now."

"Listen, hear that sound?" I hold the phone to a window. "I've got woodpeckers. They're knocking the house apart."

She bursts into tears. "That house! I wish you'd move, but I know you can't afford to."

It's the same house we grew up in, a shambles now, but with its memories intact. Once, in the upstairs hallway, after a bitter game of Monopoly, Odette and I fought with fists and fingernails. I slammed the Monopoly board down on her head; she chopped at my stomach with the side of her hand. We hurt each other enough to stop, scared at being so close to killing.

When our parents moved to Florida, my husband and I bought the house. He's different, my husband. Tim. He can actually purr. And he saves up funny things that happen to him during the day, to laugh about at night. I'll wake up and hear him laughing beside me in bed. He doesn't know or care about fixing anything that breaks, and the house is going the way of Lazarus, the car. Tim goes off on business trips and stays away longer and longer. Longer and longer. I bet he has another wife somewhere, maybe even kids.

These days, the woodpeckers are winning. The house belongs to them.

Our parents started Odette and me on this memory thing. They'd take a tray and fill it with small objects: pencil, rock, coin, cookie, Kleenex, twelve or fifteen things like that. We'd study the tray; then they'd take it away and we'd try to write everything down. Odette and I competed in that game, as we competed in everything. We lived each other's lives, then.

I still can't believe I graduated from college. Because of science, I didn't think I would. I had to take astronomy. It was grand to stare through that telescope at Jupiter, Saturn, and the Moon, but on paper it was just a math class and worse. I could never calculate the distance to a star. I was failing. The short, globular professor terrified me. He instructed the class to record the positions of the Moon and planets for a month. It was my last hope of passing, but I let the evenings slip by, recording nothing, telling myself I'd just remember when and where the Moon rose. The night before the project was due, I painted an elaborate series of pictures in watercolor and tempera, *all absolutely made up*, and submitted them in despair. Yet I passed! Either the professor took pity on me, *or else I tricked him*. Saved by art. Invention, the Beeline to Success.

Odette and I think it's funny that after our struggles with school and our dislike of teachers, that's what we became: teachers. She of voice, I of film. Childhood was a welter of lessons, as our parents gambled their money on our massive indifference. Horseback riding. The ponies threw their necks to the ground, chutelike, so that Odette and I slid off and banged the dirt with our fannies. Crocheting: our hooks tortured the yarn into traps, while the teacher, an elderly neighbor, mumbled over sweat-colored doilies. And dancing lessons.

Dancing lessons! They were wonderful. With Eva Hacek, she of the wild Czechoslovakian folksongs, the amber hair, her long neck ringed with coils of amber beads, her anger a blaze that our clumsy heels could never stomp out. She read our minds. She knew how mean spirited our souls were: "Sulking, furtive girls!" The wicked ponies and senile crochet teacher had nothing on her. Her power sprang from sex, and Odette and I knew it, obeyed it, understood it like our own names. Her shiny studio floor reflected us up to our knees. Her kitchen, behind a beaded curtain, smelled of cornmeal and paprika.

Once Odette asked me: "Remember when we met her lover?"

"What! We never saw him! We used to just wonder what he'd be like."

"We did see him, Shirlie. In the spring of our last year with her. It was dark, because she'd started our lesson late—we'd had to wait—and he came in with raindrops on his hair. Handsome—a solemn ruffian. He had japonica blossoms in his hand, and he repeated our names when she introduced us. We could tell they wanted to be alone."

"Did you just dream it, Odette?"

"No! I fell in love with him. It took one second. Nobody else ever quite measured up, after that."

I couldn't believe the memory wasn't stored in my mind like a movie-still.

Odette said, "You were in love with him too. You were fifteen and I was thirteen. We talked about him for weeks. You drew his picture and we traded it back and forth under each other's pillows."

Anybody I love, I love forever. So how could I have forgotten him?

"His name was Stephen," Odette offered.

I believed her, but I didn't remember.

This I do know: Eva Hacek grew older. She lost her studio and was reduced to running the children's square dances at a makeshift playground near the tobacco factories. One summer I worked at the Philip Morris factory; when my shift let out in the evenings, I'd see the playground pavilion all lit up and hear calliope music clunking away, the piping trebles and nasal bass, while on the stage the children marched in pairs toward Eva. With great bold gestures of her arms she separated them right and left into two perfect spirals of children who then merged and paired and swept around her again, regular as surf. A ruined fertility figure, she'd grown heavy. You can tell when somebody is poor. Once I waited until the dance was over and called out her name, but she was aloof and seemed to think I was there to pick up a son or daughter. Not long after that I read in the paper that she had died.

Now I wonder what she thought about as she guided the dancing children. Was she remembering Stephen's voice, his caresses and goodbyes? Did she ever once think of Odette and me?

The lanterns on the pavilion were purple. The calliope tunes would have stayed on her mind when she got home late and lay down to sleep. Those tunes stayed on my mind all day while I worked on cigarettes.

I remember them still.

ILLINOIS SHORT FICTION

Crossings by Stephen Minot
A Season for Unnatural Causes by Philip F. O'Connor
Curving Road by John Stewart
Such Waltzing Was Not Easy by Gordon Weaver

Rolling All the Time by James Ballard
Love in the Winter by Daniel Curley
To Byzantium by Andrew Fetler
Small Moments by Nancy Huddleston Packer

One More River by Lester Goldberg
The Tennis Player by Kent Nelson
A Horse of Another Color by Carolyn Osborn
The Pleasures of Manhood by Robley Wilson, Jr.

The New World by Russell Banks
The Actes and Monuments by John William Corrington
Virginia Reels by William Hoffman
Up Where I Used to Live by Max Schott

The Return of Service by Jonathan Baumbach
On the Edge of the Desert by Gladys Swan
Surviving Adverse Seasons by Barry Targan
The Gasoline Wars by Jean Thompson

Desirable Aliens by John Bovey
Naming Things by H. E. Francis
Transports and Disgraces by Robert Henson
The Calling by Mary Gray Hughes

Into the Wind by Robert Henderson
Breaking and Entering by Peter Makuck
The Four Corners of the House by Abraham Rothberg
Ladies Who Knit for a Living by Anthony E. Stockanes

Pastorale by Susan Engberg
Home Fires by David Long
The Canyons of Grace by Levi Peterson
Babaru by B. Wongar

Bodies of the Rich by John J. Clayton
Music Lesson by Martha Lacy Hall
Fetching the Dead by Scott R. Sanders
Some of the Things I Did Not Do by Janet Beeler Shaw

Honeymoon by Merrill Joan Gerber
Tentacles of Unreason by Joan Givner
The Christmas Wife by Helen Norris
Getting to Know the Weather by Pamela Painter

Birds Landing by Ernest Finney
Serious Trouble by Paul Friedman
Tigers in the Wood by Rebecca Kavaler
The Greek Generals Talk by Phillip Parotti

Singing on the Titanic by Perry Glasser
Legacies by Nancy Potter
Beyond This Bitter Air by Sarah Rossiter
Scenes from the Homefront by Sara Vogan

Tumbling by Kermit Moyer
Water into Wine by Helen Norris
The Trojan Generals Talk by Phillip Parotti
Playing with Shadows by Gloria Whelan

Man Without Memory by Richard Burgin
The People Down South by Cary C. Holladay
Bodies at Sea by Erin McGraw
Falling Free by Barry Targan